# Chasing Ghosts

Justin Boote

Copyright © 2022 by Justin Boote

All rights reserved.

No part of this book may be reproduced in any form or by any electronic or mechanical means, including information storage and retrieval systems, without written permission from the author, except for the use of brief quotations in a book review.

This is a work of fiction. Names, characters, places, and incidents either are the product of the author's imagination or are used fictitiously. Any resemblance to actual persons, living or dead, events, or locales is entirely coincidental.

Edited by Rachel Eastwood and Heather Ann Larson

Formatted by Horrorsmith Editing.

# Get Your Free Book!

GET YOUR FREE BOOK!

https://dl.bookfunnel.com/b00dfjcobx

# One

He saw the young girl walking along the side of the road by herself, and once again his body reacted of its own accord. His heart took a direct leap to his throat, bobbing frantically as though trying to play tag with his Adam's apple. The tingling sensation in the bottom of his stomach made him shift on the car's seat, as if his bowels were planning an unscheduled evacuation. It wasn't a bad feeling, though; in fact, one he had come to look forward to, the timing so unpredictable, like the almost forgotten sun peering through heavy clouds after a long spate of storms. But he never forgot; the episodes had taken up residence in the forefront of his mind since the very first time he had this feeling. They controlled his every action, haunted and tormented his dreams, until unable to resist any longer he was compelled to answer their call.

He was no longer in possession of his faculties. Another had taken his place—his very own doppelganger, casting his habitual persona to one side so all he could do was sit back and watch. It certainly didn't feel like he was doing these things himself, only savouring the aftermath, replaying the events in his mind while his 'other' took all the chances. Even if he could have a hand in matters, he wouldn't have cared about risks—the prize was too great for such trivialities.

As he slowed down, checking his rear-view mirror to ensure no one was coming, his heart took another leap when he recognised her. She was someone he had been thinking about for a while now. The girl with that domineering arsehole of a father. Believing himself to be superior to everyone else, just because he owned a big, fancy building company. The number of times he had fantasised about getting rid of him, to make his life easier, after their arguments, his interference, as if he was running the show in this community. Maybe it wouldn't be a bad idea to do something about that. Once the girl was taken care of, naturally.

Suzy looked behind her, no doubt worried about the slowing car, assuming her father had warned her about strangers, but he was no stranger. She had known him all her life. It was a small village—everyone knew everyone.

The smile he used in such cases stretched itself across his face. His muscles in such situations were always tight, making it hard to perform simple actions. There was the danger of his body betraying him, forming the wrong expression on his face. Cold, tight lips saying the wrong word, spooking her, as he would try to coax her into his car. It shouldn't be the case tonight, though. Tonight it should be easier than ever.

"Hey there, Suzy! What are you doing out by yourself at this time of night? Does your father know where you are?"

"Hi! Yes, it's okay. I texted him a while ago. It was my friend's birthday, so he let me stay out a bit longer."

Suzy had to be about fourteen by now. She was becoming a young woman, but even so, he couldn't believe her father had let her walk home alone so late at night. The man must be getting soft in his old age. The thought made him chuckle. The only thing that would make him soft would be the putrefaction of his body as he wasted away in his coffin.

"Let me give you a ride home. It's cold out here. C'mon, hop in."

"It's okay, really. I don't mind the walk and listening to my music. I'm nearly home anyway."

"Nonsense. Come on. You know most accidents and, umm, incidents, occur within a one-mile radius of the victim's homes, right? It's true, you know. I would hate to go off and, when I read the paper tomorrow…"

He let the words hang, hoping she would take the bait. The muscles on his face were starting to ache now with this fake smile still plastered there.

*Bitch. Just get in the damn car.*

Suzy seemed to consider her options, perhaps trying to think of another feasible excuse, although she shouldn't have any. There was no reason for her to be afraid of him—not in her mind, at least. And besides, he wasn't lying—it *was* cold. All the more reason for the little bitch to get in. So far he'd been fortunate; not a single car had driven past but that could change at any second. Bradwell might be a small village, and few people would be about this late at night, but in a way, that made it even more dangerous.

He was starting to get nervous now as a result. His smile was starting to twitch, on the verge of cracking under the pressure. His hands were closing into fists of their own accord. If he had to get out and grab her, he was going to be really pissed. One had to be calm and collected; if not, that's how mistakes were made.

Suzy continued weighing up her options, looking around, debating with herself. He shouldn't have been surprised; the village was aware of the spate of attacks on girls in the area over the last few months. Another reason her father shouldn't have let her walk home. Just as he thought he would have to get out of the car and drag her to the back seat, she smiled back at him.

"Okay, sure. Thanks!"

Suzy got in the passenger seat.

He was visibly trembling with anticipation. He gripped the steering wheel hard so she wouldn't notice, forcing deep breaths out through his nose. It was a good thing he was wearing his jacket or she might have seen his heart pummelling against his chest.

"Great," he forced through sudden dry lips. "Let's go. You might have frozen to death out there."

Suzy said nothing, only smiling back at him. Good. He didn't want to get in a conversation with her, either—he didn't think he was truly capable of speaking more than a few monosyllabic words right now. He pulled away, going slowly so as not to make her suspect anything was wrong, even though his desire was to roar off at top speed to his intended location. *Just keep calm*, he told himself like a chant. *Just like all the other times.*

Suzy seemed happy to listen to the music she had playing through her earphones, so he said nothing and drove. They came to a crossroads—Suzy's house was to the left. He turned right. Glancing at her out of the corner of his eye, he saw her suddenly sit up, staring back out of the window as she saw her street vanishing behind her. She pulled out one of the earphones. *Here we go...*

"Hey, I think you made a mistake. We're going in the wrong direction."

Her voice had a distinct edge to it, somehow squeakier, hurried. Maybe for a second the possibility it hadn't been a simple mistake on his behalf entered her thoughts.

"It's okay," he said quickly, smiling at her again. "I just need to check on something before I take you home. Won't be a second."

The last thing he needed was for her to start screaming, or as had happened before, to open the door and jump out while the car was still in motion. That had been scary.

"But...but where are we going? I need to get home. My dad will kill me. I should be home by now."

"It's alright. I'll speak to your father when we arrive and explain things. I'm a good client of his. This is rather important, something I only just remembered."

"Please, can't it wait? Take me home first."

"Sorry, I can't."

The car left the village. He drove past a couple of fields on either side of the road until they came to where a small woodland area began—Fritton Woods. Suzy was visibly agitated now, constantly asking, begging him to turn around and take her home, but it was too late for that now. If he had been in possession of his own faculties, he might have considered it—after all, he'd known her all her life—but he wasn't anymore.

They reached the small opening he now knew so well and turned down a rugged dirt track. At the bottom he stopped the car and turned off the engine. He turned to Suzy, who was already fumbling with her phone, sobbing quietly and shaking her head, because, really, this couldn't be happening, could it? Kids were told not to get in stranger's cars and he wasn't a stranger, but why else would they be out here in the middle of nowhere?

"I want to go home," she sobbed as she began to search for her father's number in her phone.

"Sorry, Suzy, but that can't happen."

He took out the knife from the inside of his jacket and punched it into Suzy's chest. An hour later he drove home whistling to himself. His other self had finally gone, allowing the real him back again. He went straight to bed—he had an idea it might be a long day tomorrow and he was going to need his strength.

# Two

Angela Harford and her partner, Doug Ramsey, arrived at 11 Parkland Drive, their siren blaring, blue lights flashing like lightning. She parked the car outside the house and turned off the ignition. Immediately, the road regained its previous serenity before they'd turned onto it—dark and quiet with just a few streetlamps dotted along the pavement to ease neighbours' nerves and prevent the shadows from taking on a more sinister appearance. A few lights went on inside various homes, curtains tentatively pulled back and faces appeared in corners wondering what the fuss might be, but not showing their faces too much in case they were implicated in some way. Others peered from bedroom windows. It was the kind of road—a cul-de-sac—that suggested flashing blue lights and police sirens were a rarity. Gardens were nicely kept, houses freshly painted, expensive cars parked outside each home.

Except this one.

It looked as though it had been dumped here unceremoniously, by an alien race, because it was so conspicuous in its complete and utter lack of upkeep and maintenance. The windows were grimy and dusty, which was obvious even at night. The garden was a well-developed home for weeds, some a few feet high already, so thick it might have harboured the odd snake and rat nests. The paint had cracked exposing brickwork underneath, and it was quite difficult to determine what colour the house had originally been painted. It belonged more in another part of town, where people did not have cars parked outside their homes—unless they were old and rusty, maybe missing a wheel or two. The kind of street where at this time of night—after midnight—there would be suspicious-looking kids hanging on street corners, swapping notes for drugs. It immediately caught Angela's attention and made her wonder if the call they had received only moments before was actually real rather than a prank. The place looked haunted.

"What do you think?" she asked Doug.

He shrugged his shoulders in a non-committed way as he scanned the house. "Dunno, looks pretty creepy, so wouldn't surprise me if the call was real. We're here, anyway."

Yes, they were here, but Angela was feeling like this was going to be a huge waste of time. Time that could have been spent at home with her daughter, Kim. Fortunately, it was her last time working the graveyard shift. She hoped so, at least.

"Well, let's go check it out. If it's a prank call, you're paying for coffee."

"Let's hope it's a prank, then. Bored kids with nothing better to do. I'm ready for bed as it is."

"Amen to that."

Angela radioed dispatch to tell them they were at the scene and were proceeding to knock on the door. They both climbed out, aware of more eyes on them, the occasional door now open with men in their dressing gowns staring out. It was cold out here for October, the northerly wind skating down the road making Angela's skin break out in goosebumps. For the umpteenth time, she cursed the desk sergeant for putting her on the night shift patrol. *One more night*, she told herself. *One more night*.

"Okay, let's do this."

They headed down the garden path, hearing things rustle among the dense weeds, hoping it wasn't rats ready to jump at their throats. It seemed the kind of thing one would expect in a place like this.

Angela knocked on the door and took a step back, assuming the house was abandoned and kids had played a prank, probably watching them from behind a car, stifling giggles. Assumed, because the call had sounded like a joke. If it were true, she expected to see people shouting and screaming, lights on everywhere, neighbours standing outside in the street, but there was none of that.

She sighed, ready to knock again, then remind Doug it was his turn to pay for coffee at the all-nighter not too far away, when to her surprise the door opened. She had been so sure it was a prank that her arm stopped in mid-air before she could knock again. It looked as though she was waving to someone.

A man in his night clothes stood there, as harmless as could be, yet his eyes and corkscrew black hair betrayed his sense of innocence. If it wasn't for the spots of blood on his face and dressing gown, Angela might have thought she'd just woke the poor guy from a deep sleep.

"Mr Tennant? We received a call that there had been an... incident," she said, already on alert.

*Please tell me they made a mistake. Please don't let it be true.*

"Umm, yes, please, follow me."

His wife appeared beside him, looking like she'd just witnessed some terrible event—her long, brown hair was just as ruffled, eyes puffy and bloodshot and hands visibly shaking. Her whole body, in fact, as though she was freezing to death. She clutched her husband's arm and started sobbing.

Angela cast a dubious eye at Doug, who she could tell was

thinking the same thing as her. *This cannot be. This has to be a joke*. But like her, his eyes kept glancing at the blood splatter on Mr Tennant's gown and his wife's nightie.

Mr Tennant stood aside and let them in. Suddenly edgy and apprehensive, Angela and Doug stepped inside, both scanning the house for... what, Angela wasn't entirely sure. And yet, the moment Angela entered a chill ran through her, goosebumps broke on her arms. It was as if she had been smothered by a cold blanket. One left in the freezer all night. Something flashed through her mind, the beginnings of a headache gnawed at her skull, as if someone was probing her memories. A sudden image of her dead brother, Jimmy, appeared and disappeared just as abruptly. Angela shivered and focused her attention on the couple before her.

Neither of the Tennants gave any indication of having mental issues or were the kind of people who might have done what they had claimed to on the phone. They weren't screaming and howling as should be the case, either—something was not right.

"So, on the phone we were told that there had been a—"

"Yes, yes. I'll take you to her. Follow me."

Angela had only been on the force for nine months but had already learned that '*trust no one*' was a mantra to be repeated on every call, no matter how minor it seemed. You never knew if the call you were responding to had been perpetrated by someone with mental problems, or an underlying issue with the police force itself, someone high on drugs that was not in their right mind anymore. In other words, the most innocent-looking person could turn on you in an instant. For that reason, they both made sure Mr and Mrs Tennant stayed in front of them, and the two officers had one hand hovering over their truncheons while their eyes scanned every shadow and dark corner where someone could be lying in wait for them. It wouldn't be the first time.

Soon after Angela started patrolling she responded to a call from a woman complaining her neighbour's dog barked incessantly day and night. She confronted him and threatened to poison the damn thing if he didn't make it stop. His reply in no uncertain terms was what would happen if she went anywhere near his dog. The woman started shouting abuse and the neighbour, an elderly gentleman nearing his eighties, returned the insults. Angela was caught completely off guard when she stepped between them in an attempt to mediate and he smacked her on the nose, breaking it instantly. The next day, fellow officers had laughed about it, as had she in hindsight, but the warning had been there and she had never forgotten it.

The Tennants took them to a door under the stairs and Angela's suspicions were raised even higher. There was nothing to indicate a fight had occurred, nothing was out of place, no blood anywhere except on their clothes. He turned on the light to the basement and pointed.

"She...she's down there," he said, his voice croaky, bottom lip quivering. Mrs Tennant was still sobbing, holding on tightly to her husband's arm.

"Who's down there?" asked Doug.

Both officers looked at each other, dismay and uncertainty in their eyes. Angela was still hesitant about going down there and leaving the Tennants up here, so she told them to go down first. For all she knew, they might want to kidnap them for whatever reason, hold them to ransom. Terrorists came in all guises these days.

They didn't have to go down far to confirm their worst suspicions. The call dispatch received had been from a sobbing man telling them he had just killed his fourteen-year-old daughter and could they please send someone over. She lay in a growing pool of blood, sprawled on the floor.

Automatisms instantly sprang into action in both officers. They bolted down the remaining steps and knelt beside her, careful not to get any blood on themselves. When Doug checked her pulse then shook his head, Angela radioed back to dispatch, keeping one eye on the girl's parents, who remained holding each other halfway down the stairs, as if they dared not get any closer.

It became clear the parents had no intentions of locking them down there with the girl—instead, the arrival of the police and checking her pulse had confirmed this wasn't a nightmare, the mother burst into hysterical sobs of despair—Angela set in motion the next steps by confirming the call hadn't been a prank. She was told not to touch anything, the crew was on its way. She agreed and hung up.

She wasn't entirely sure what to do at this point. The girl's parents were both inconsolable, hugging each other tightly, looking more like victims than instigators of this terrible tragedy. She really didn't want to have to put handcuffs on them but knew she had no choice. Assuming they weren't going to do anything stupid, she approached them, Doug beside her.

"What happened? Why?" was all she could muster. There was a sob caught in her own throat; this was the worst possible scenario a mother could imagine—killing one's own child.

Neither of the Tennants said anything, staring down at the bloodied body of their daughter as if in total shock and disbelief. The scene was surreal in its gruesome nature—the girl had been stabbed what appeared to be multiple times in the stomach. What could possibly…

In the distance she could already hear the sound of sirens approaching. Soon this would be declared a crime scene, all the neighbours would be standing outside in the road asking questions. The same questions Angela was asking herself.

"Why Mr Tennant? Why did you do it?"

Of the two, he looked the most composed, albeit barely. His wife looked on the verge of fainting.

"I had to. I had no choice," he muttered.

"But why?" she asked again. "What did she do for you to kill her?"

As if the question was confirmation of what they had done, a shriek burst from his wife's lips, her legs wobbled, and she collapsed. Mr Tennant quickly grabbed her and held her tight.

"I'm afraid we're going to have to arrest you both," said Doug. He read them their rights. "You don't seem the type of people to do such a thing. What on earth made you do it?"

"I had to," he repeated. "I didn't have a choice. It was that or she would have suffered more. It was the only option we had. That or she suffered more."

He stifled a sob, but his eyes were wide and furious. His jaw stuck out as he gritted his teeth, his hands curled into fists.

"Who made you do this, Mr Tennant? Was there an intruder? Someone with a grudge in retaliation for something?" asked Angela.

He wasn't making any sense. How and why would anyone possibly force them to have stabbed their daughter to death?

There was a loud knock on the front door, like someone was hitting it with a hammer, then it burst open.

"I'll go," said Doug. He dashed past the Tennants, still on the stairs, and went to greet the detectives.

"Who, Mr Tennant?" she asked.

"He made us do it," sobbed Mrs Tennant. "That thing in our house."

# Three

"What happened?" asked a plain-clothes officer as he stepped down into the basement.

"We were called to the scene after the Tennants here phoned to say they had murdered their daughter. As you can see, it wasn't a prank as we first suspected," said Doug.

The detective surveyed the basement, cast suspicious eyes at the Tennants, and shook his head.

"You admit to doing this, do you?" he asked, his voice rough, like he was barking out the questions.

Mr Tennant nodded.

"Why? Why'd you do it? What did she do to you?"

Mr Tennant said nothing, merely shaking his head. The detective turned to Doug, eyebrows raised, waiting for an answer.

"He, umm, said that they were made to do it. Someone forced them to kill her."

The detective cast a conspiratorial glance and rubbed the stubble of his beard.

Angela didn't know who he was or his exact rank, but she guessed he was old enough to be her father. The wrinkles on his face; and the receding grey hair were good enough indicators. She wondered if it was stress or the natural passage of time that had caused him to look older than his years.

"Who made you do it, Mr Tennant?" he barked.

The man ignored him. Instead, he kissed his wife's forehead and drew her closer. Again, the detective glared at Doug in his *well-are-you-gonna-tell-me* stare.

"They refused to tell us, Sir."

"Mmm. Not surprised. Didn't think we'd be coming back to this house again. Alright, take them to the station. We'll wait for the crime scene unit to get here."

Doug and Angela led the Tennants away to their car. Angela was confused. There had been a look in the detective's eyes that suggested he wasn't entirely unfamiliar with what had just happened—as if it was another routine *'parents killed their kid'* scenario. And what he had said about not expecting to return to this house. What did that mean?

In the back of the police car no one said anything —the only sounds were the roar of the engine and the Tennant's sobbing. Angela's head was reeling, a dozen questions colliding in her head, each one appearing before she could even attempt at answering the previous. Once at the station they escorted the couple to separate cells, which produced another bout of hysteria from Mrs Tennant, not wanting to be separated from her husband. It took nearly ten minutes for Mrs Tennant to understand they had no choice in the matter, but Doug promised to try and get them out as soon as possible. Which wasn't going to happen.

The desk sergeant contacted their lawyers, leaving Doug and Angela near the end of their shifts. But Angela didn't want to leave. What the wife had said still swam in her mind like a trapped soul. Along with the words of the plain clothes detective.

"You want that coffee?" asked Doug.

"Yeah, sure."

They went to the kitchen area and Angela sat down while waiting for Doug to make the drinks. She held her head in her hands, processing everything that had just happened, ensuring she had heard the woman correctly.

"Here," said Doug, making her jump as he handed her a coffee mug.

"Thanks."

She took a sip and the heat burned the insides of her mouth then throat as it travelled down to her stomach. She relished it, though—as if washing away the poison that seemed to be burning away in her intestines. This was Bradwell, a tiny village on the east coast of England, and while its history was plenty gruesome enough, a couple killing their daughter in apparent cold blood and being treated by the detective as though a minor offence made her feel sick. There had to be something she was missing.

"What do you think?" she asked after waiting for the burning in her throat to dissipate.

"Me? I don't have a damn clue. I've been an officer for three years and I have never seen anything so...bizarre. What the hell were they talking about? Someone made them do it? And tell me you agree when I say they do not look like a couple who murdered their daughter voluntarily, or come across as cold-blooded killers?"

"No, they don't. Far from it. If I didn't know any better, I would have said they were just as shocked and horrified as you would expect from parents who just found their daughter brutally murdered. Someone made them do it. Maybe the father is a secret gambler, owed someone money, I dunno. Daughter was caught up in something, not as innocent as they believed her to be, and someone came for her? But to admit to it, stabbing her to death? You saw the wife—she fainted.

"And what was that the detective said? About not being surprised? What was all that about?"

"I have no idea," replied Doug as he resumed drinking his coffee.

Angela didn't either. There had been something in that house that had made her flesh crawl. A sensation of being watched, as if there was someone else in the basement with them. Could there have been and the couple was covering for them? It felt as if multiple eyes were scrutinising her, reading her very thoughts. Boring into her soul. It made her shiver just thinking about it. Maybe because it wasn't the first time it had happened to her.

"What do you think will happen to them?" asked Doug, jerking her from her thoughts.

"Huh? I don't know. If they have a good lawyer and they continue saying the same thing, he might get them admitted to Northgate Hospital for the Mentally Impaired for a while. Even the other one, for the Criminally Insane. Who knows? But before that happens, I want to speak to them again. Why don't we try and do so before their lawyer gets here? Now they're away from that house, they might want to open up a bit more. I got the impression they were almost afraid to speak while still there. As if someone was listening."

"Yeah. Me, too. Like there was someone else in the basement with us. Creepy as shit. I just wanted to get the hell out of there."

So she hadn't been the only one with the same sensation. She didn't want to tell Doug— they hadn't been partners for very long and the level of confidence wasn't quite there, yet— but in a way it made her feel better. For years she had been questioning herself about these little insights she sometimes had, sensing things around her that were not necessarily of this world, but she'd never had anyone to discuss it with except her ex-husband, and look how that turned out. Her mother had told her when she was young that she sometimes sensed things in people and certain areas and Angela assumed she had picked it up from her. It didn't make it any easier to understand, though—she often wondered if a spell at Northgate was required for herself, too.

"I'm going to go speak to the wife," she said, pretending to ignore his comment. "Why don't you speak to the husband?"

Doug agreed and they headed towards the holding cells. Angela could hear Mrs Tennant sobbing in her cell. Again, she thought of her daughter, Kim, currently at home with Angela's mother, who stayed over when she had to work nights. She loved her more than anything else in the world, making her wonder what could possibly drive someone to commit such a despicable act.

She opened the cell door and stepped in, the woman's slight frame and build making her look even more fragile in this cold, inhospitable room. Angela smiled, despite the bitterness in her heart and heavy weight in her stomach, wanting the woman to feel like she was here to help her, not judge or condemn her for what she had done.

"Hi, how you holding up? I'm sure your lawyer will be here soon. Can I get you a coffee or anything in the meantime? It tastes like mud, but it's hot at least."

"No, I'm fine, thank you. I guess we'll both be going to prison for life, won't we? I understand if that's the case. Anyone who kills their child in cold blood should. That's what I think anyway. That or reintroduce the death penalty."

*Then why did you do it?*

"Mrs Tennant, I—"

"Please, call me Margaret."

"Okay, Margaret, I have no idea how things will turn out. All I do know is that this is a terrible tragedy and I want to understand why and how it happened. You said something about being forced to do it. Someone made you do it. Can you tell me, just between the two of us, what you meant? I have a fourteen-year-old daughter myself. I just want to know why."

She looked at the poor woman in more detail now that they were alone. Margaret bore all the physical signs of someone clinically depressed and suffering from a chronic, incurable illness. Her unpainted fingernails were practically non-existent, bitten down to raw flesh. Even from here Angela could smell her breath—as though she'd been eating rotten meat for the last few days. Her permed, brown hair looked exactly like an abandoned bird's nest on the top of her head and her eyes were rheumy and glazed. She'd evidently spent a lot of time biting her lower lip, too, because it was scabby and sore-looking. She was fidgeting constantly, wringing her hands together, unable to look Angela in the eyes for too long.

"Margaret?" she prompted again.

"He made us do it," she whispered, glancing around the cell, as if the perpetrator might be listening.

"Who, Margaret? Who? Tell me and I'll arrest him right now. Was it someone your husband was involved with? On the file it says he was an accountant. Did someone feel wronged by him somehow and wanted revenge?"

She snorted. A horrible sound reminiscent of a neighing horse. Snot dripped from her nostrils. She shook her head.

"Look, Margaret. I think someone who was evidently upset with you both for whatever reason made you kill your daughter. If that's the case, you need to tell me. Or at least your lawyer. It will help in the trial. If you don't tell us, you'll spend the rest of your life in prison."

Margaret looked up and stared Angela in the eye. "Don't you get it? Our daughter is dead. We killed her. Do you think I give a shit what happens to me now? I want to die, I can't spend the rest of my life knowing what we did. So I don't care about the trial or spending the rest of my life in prison. Hopefully while I'm there someone will put me out of my misery. And if I tell you who did it, you'll think I'm mad anyway, and no one will believe us."

"Then what difference does it make if you tell me or not? It's all the same, you just said so yourself."

"*He* made us do it."

She almost spat the word at Angela and held her head in her hands and started sobbing again. Before Angela could continue pressing her, the door opened and a tall, thin man wearing a suit and tie and carrying a briefcase stepped in.

"Don't say another word."

Exasperated, yet feeling she was getting nowhere, Angela left Margaret with her lawyer, hoping she would confide in him instead, and went to see if Doug had better luck.

She found him already in the kitchen, sipping from another coffee cup and took this to be a bad sign.

"Let me guess," she said, "he told you he was made to do it but wouldn't say who?"

"Correct. I gave up after about five minutes. No point insisting. Maybe his lawyer can get it out of him, but in the meantime, while you were gone, I did a quick check on the database. You're going to like this."

"What? And make it good—I want to go home."

"Oh, it is. The Tennants are not the only ones to kill their daughter in that house. From the quick search I did, there's at least another five over the last thirty years. All parents that killed their daughters in cold blood and refused to give a motive."

# Four

It was early morning when Angela returned home. Her head was spinning and despite how tired she was, she had an idea it would be a long time before she managed to get some well-earned sleep. As always, she checked on Kim before getting out of her uniform and putting her pyjamas on. She lingered longer than usual this time, not wanting to wake her, yet at the same time she had an almost overwhelming desire to get in bed beside her and hug her. Hug her tightly and tell her over and over how much she loved her. She wasn't too surprised to find tears welling in her eyes as she watched the sleeping girl's chest rise and fall mechanically. The poor kid. After everything she had been through and imagining what the Tennant's daughter must have suffered, Angela realised just how lucky they actually were.

Only that morning Kim had asked about Terry, her father, who she hadn't seen or heard from in over three months. It broke Angela's heart every time the subject was brought up, and at just fourteen Angela wasn't quite willing to give her the real reasons for their breakup and subsequent divorce. All Kim knew was that her job took up too much time and Terry got fed up with only seeing her sporadically. He'd met someone eight months ago at the marketing firm he worked at, and when Angela refused to reconsider her chosen career, he had left. That had been bad enough, but it seemed he had decided to break all ties with them, meaning he hardly ever visited or phoned. The last Angela heard he was living in Scotland somewhere.

In a way she could understand why Terry had decided to look elsewhere for company—the job was indeed tiring and stressful, meaning she had little energy for Terry at the end of a shift. That, and a young teenager to contend with had been the catalysts. But to abandon his daughter, who had cried for weeks afterwards when he never bothered to phone on her fourteenth birthday, Kim had begun to wonder if it had been her fault. Nothing Angela said could convince her otherwise, and she had to concede it must seem that way after the man had practically disowned her.

But the real reason—or at least another important one—were her nightmares that would wake them both in the middle of the night, when she started screaming, covered in a cold sweat. The way she knew things about his day that she couldn't possibly know. Sometimes what he was thinking while in the shower or making dinner. He said it was creepy and not normal and it felt like being violated—psychologically. She tried to explain it was nothing bad, it was a kind of sixth sense she sometimes picked up on. Like her mother. It was later when Angela discovered he was seeing the secretary she figured he must have got paranoid and scared.

But Kim didn't need to know these things. Now, after what Angela had seen over at that house, Kim needed protecting more than ever; hers and the love from her mother who was sleeping in the spare bedroom. She quietly closed Kim's door, went to her bedroom and got changed, and headed downstairs for a glass of wine, hoping this might knock her out sufficiently so she could sleep without thinking of that poor girl, lying in a pool of her own blood. The wine did send her to sleep, but her dreams were not peaceful ones, but slight deviations of the nightmares that had plagued almost her whole life.

In this nightmare, as in all the previous ones, she was with her younger brother, Jimmy. She had been forced to act as a motherly figure after their dad died of cancer when Angela was eighteen and Jimmy twelve. Their mother couldn't cope with bringing up two children and working ten hours a day, so it was Angela who ensured Jimmy did his homework, was bathed and fed each night. She also took him with her when their mother gave her money to do the weekly shopping.

She was there now with him as they meandered along the aisles, making sure they got the necessities before turning their attention to whatever cakes or biscuits the money left over permitted. Jimmy had a real sweet tooth and would spend ages staring at the assorted chocolate bars and biscuits while Angela filled the cart with toilet paper, rice, pasta, cleaning products, whatever meat and fish she figured she could cook easily. There was a commotion, someone shouting, then a scream—always that bloodcurdling scream that should have told her what was happening. Her initial thought was a fight, perhaps someone had run off without paying. It was that hesitation, not going immediately to Jimmy, that caused everything else to happen afterwards and even now, all these years later.

More shouting and screaming and yelling ensued, making Angela nervous. She quickly went to find Jimmy when there was a loud bang, like thunder rumbling right here in the supermarket. It made her drop the bottle of milk she had been holding and it shattered on the floor. The woman that had been screaming was suddenly quiet, as if someone had clamped a hand over her mouth. Angela hurried towards her brother. She saw him standing in the centre of the aisle, looking at the entrance. A man was standing there wearing a clown mask. This was the focal point of another recurring nightmare of hers. She hated clowns ever since, couldn't bear to be near them. The man was holding what looked like a double-barrel shotgun. She could see wisps of smoke rising from the end of the barrels like tiny, fleeing spectres. On the floor next to him was a woman, sprawled out, a growing pool of blood spreading out from underneath her. Her body was twitching. A leg, then an arm, while the pool continued growing like an oil slick on the sea.

She might have screamed or called for Jimmy to get the hell out of the way and run to the back exit, but she couldn't remember. What she did remember—and dreamt about night after night —was seeing the man turn towards Jimmy. They seemed to regard each other for a while, contemplate one another, and then something sparked in Jimmy and he screamed. And as he screamed the man in the clown mask raised his smoking shotgun and blasted a hole in Jimmy's face, showering Angela in flesh, bone and brain matter. Some of it went in her open mouth, and she swallowed as her brain tried to comprehend what had just happened.

She looked from her brother to the clown then back to her brother again, trying to decide which one she should go to. When she looked up again the clown man was already sprinting out the door. Only then did reality kick in.

But now the nightmare—the replaying of that real event all those years ago—changed slightly. Instead of rushing to Jimmy's side, screaming and howling for help before cradling her baby brother's body, not caring that she was covering herself in his sticky blood and gore, he twitched, and the one half of his face that hadn't been blown off twitched. His remaining eye opened and stared at her with cold, vitriolic hatred. He tried to say something, but his tongue was missing and his lower jaw was bouncing off his chest. So instead, he grabbed her, surprisingly strong despite his life source puddling beneath them, and tried to pull her closer. Perhaps he wanted to whisper something in her ear, tell her he loved her and to say the same to Mum, but as her face was dragged ever closer to his and she could smell the coppery stench around them he managed to somehow gargle into her ear words she could barely understand but knew the implications regardless.

"You let me die. My big sister let me die."

And while she screamed, hysterical, shaking her head in denial of the facts, he clutched her tightly and pulled himself to his feet. He stood there, swaying on wobbly legs, his one, cyclopean eye accusing her, his arms reaching for her, lumps of flesh and bone falling to the floor from the glistening hole in his face, a garbled moan coming from shattered lips. Normally Angela would wake at this moment, screaming herself hoarse at the implications of what Jimmy had said, but this time; there was something else in this recurring nightmare. At the entrance to the supermarket a shadow grew like the pool of blood beneath them, taking on a human form until she recognised the slight features of her daughter, Kim, standing there smiling in all her innocence. And it was only when Jimmy saw her, and headed in that direction instead, did Angela wake up and clap a hand over her mouth to prevent the scream from escaping.

# Five

It was supposed to be Angela's day off; tomorrow she would be back with Doug on the day shift, the safest shift. But a large part of her was incapable of drawing her mind away from the events at 11 Parkland Drive. What Margaret had told her, then subsequently what Doug had added.

*At least another five more over the last thirty years.*

It seemed impossible that such a thing could occur outside of a horror movie or a news story she heard in some faraway country. Perhaps one of those ghastly stories by the authors Terry used to like reading that always gave her the creeps. But for it to happen here in her own backyard, and even more inexplicably to have happened not just once before but *five times*? That had to be more than coincidence, surely. She would readily admit the house looked the perfect setting for such a gruesome event to occur, as though haunted, but that was just her imagination playing with her, despite a growing sensation in the back of her mind that suggested it wasn't. If it were true, the house would surely have been demolished, burnt down by superstitious neighbours. She would have heard about it from fellow officers when they returned to the station. But it was as if the subject had been deliberately hushed, perhaps to avoid attention in the area, or quite simply, it was such a terrible occurrence to have happened repeatedly, that by pretending it never happened it would all blow over and be forgotten.

Well, not anymore. Angela had every intention of finding out the history of that place and what could possibly have caused these things to occur.

There was also last night.

When she had woken with her hand clamped firmly over her mouth, the blanket half lying on the floor as if she'd been fighting for real in her sleep, it had taken her a long time to comprehend this new development in her tortuous routine. Until now it always ended with Jimmy reaching out for her, blaming her for letting him die like that. In the days after Jimmy's death, her mother had implied the same thing; it was in her eyes, the way she looked at Angela. The accusatory questions; *"Why didn't you protect my baby boy? You were supposed to be taking care of him and you let him die!"*

*"The guy had a gun, Mum! What did you expect me to do?"*

*"You should have done more. Hide."*

And this accusation had nearly killed Angela, too.

So why was Kim now a part of this?

As though she had heard her mother's thought, Kim strolled into the kitchen. An immediate surge of emotion shook through her body as she watched her, long blonde hair in corkscrews, face—for the only moment of the day without makeup—and wearing her yellow pyjamas. A tear brushed past her eyelashes as Kim smiled and kissed Angela on the cheek.

"Hi, Mum!" she said as she grabbed a bottle of orange juice from the fridge.

Angela could barely reply, there was a sob caught in her throat. The image of the Tennant girl's body in the basement, an innocent victim who had done nothing to deserve such a cruel end. She might have gone to the same school as Kim—

maybe they knew each other. It was totally feasible in such a small village.

"What's wrong, Mum? You look like you've been crying."

She coughed back the sob and reached out for her, wanting a hug. "It was just a tough shift at work and I'm tired. But hey, I've got the day off and back to days tomorrow. We should do something."

"Umm, Mum, I got school. It's Wednesday."

She gave Angela a look that said *something you want to tell me?* Angela laughed. After what happened last night she had lost certain basic notions, like time.

"Oops, sorry! Another day then, I guess. I could order Chinese food tonight. How's that sound?"

"I'm vegetarian, Mum. So as long as you don't get anything with meat in it."

*Shit.*

She'd forgotten about that as well. Seemed she'd forgotten a lot of things lately. Except for the dreams. They never went away.

"I know that. Where's your grandmother, anyway?"

"She left early, to go to the market. Told me last night."

Angela barely heard her. There was an image in her head of going to 11 Parkland Drive and seeing not the body of the Tennant's daughter, but Kim's. Brutally stabbed and mutilated

"I'm gonna take a shower," she replied and abruptly headed upstairs before Kim could see fresh tears appear.

She turned the water as hot as she could bear, then scrubbed herself until her flesh was nearly red raw. Subconsciously hoping she was scrubbing away the images from her nightmare. Because another part of her was already thinking about her plan for today—day off or not.

When she finished, Kim was already about to leave. She gave her another hug, told her she loved her more than anything in the world and watched her go. A thought crossed her mind—

*what if I never see her again? What if something happens to her like it did to Jimmy, or the Tennant's daughter?*

"It won't," she told the empty house.

Before her mind could conjure more morbid thoughts, she phoned Doug, wondering if he was still asleep or not. He answered quickly, suggesting he wasn't. They hadn't been partners long, but she knew that he lived alone in a rented apartment after recently separating from a long-term girlfriend. He told her he preferred to be at work rather than home so he didn't have to think about her.

"Hi, Angela. You didn't get much sleep, either?"

*I could have if I wasn't seeing my dead brother in my dreams.*

"Nope. Can't stop thinking about the case. What you said. Say, you doing anything today? I'd like to check through the old case files, maybe hit the internet on the history of the place, too."

"Your place or mine?"

She smiled. "Bit of an old-fashioned chat up line, isn't it? But anyway, I'm pretty sure you're itching to get out of there already so why not come here? You can pick up the files while you're at it."

"I'll be there in an hour."

He hung up and she smiled again. Poor guy. What kind of life was it when one preferred to work rather than be at home?

When Doug knocked she let him in and was pleasantly surprised to see him out of uniform. He looked younger than his thirty-two years, in his black jeans and cream coloured jacket. His mop of black hair might have seen a brush, maybe not, and he was already sporting a day's stubble. His green eyes were warm, not like the cold, haunted aspect they presented when they were patrolling the area. In one arm he was carrying a number of files.

"Come on in. Coffee? Something stronger?"

"What do you think I am, your typical cliché cop? The lonely alcoholic who can only get through the stresses of life with alcohol in his system?"

"I have no idea. After last night maybe a pick-me-up?"

"Well, if you've got any brandy to slip in that coffee, I won't say no," he said, looking sheepish.

"Done." She laughed.

They headed to her office and sat at the desk.

"I take it you've been thinking about what I found last night?" he asked.

"I can't stop thinking about it. It's enough that one set of parents kill their child, but five? That's not normal, Doug."

"My thoughts precisely. Like it's a bloody English Amityville. Next, we'll have ghost-hunters and haunted house tours going through the place."

He laughed nervously. Angela didn't. Doug didn't have kids so this couldn't affect him as deeply, or as personally, as it did her. Perhaps one day he would understand. He must have noticed the solemn look on her face, though, because his smile vanished.

"What? I was joking you know. You don't think..."

"No, I don't. But I have a daughter that age, Doug. I couldn't imagine how anyone could do that. Such savagery."

"Ah, right. Gotcha. Yeah, you've got a point. Does make me wonder, though. Look."

He opened the files and took out five separate sheets of paper. "First case—a couple suffocated their 13-year-old daughter to death in 1992. Three years later, in 1995, parents killed their daughter by hitting her over the head with a blunt instrument. A hammer as it later turned out. A year later, 1996. This time, stabbed to death. In 2001 a young couple strangled their 6-year-old, and lastly, until yesterday, in 2004, a man killed his daughter by throwing her down the stairs, then strangling her when the fall didn't kill her.

"Five deaths, all young girls, all murders confessed to by the parents without giving any explanation as to motive. Of the five sets of parents in these files, those that actually committed the murders are in prison serving life, another two are at Northgate Hospital for the Criminally Insane, and the last—the father who threw his daughter down the stairs—committed suicide in his cell before it got to trial. The wife or husband present at the murders received twelve years for accessory to murder. And now we have a sixth case. Identical in every aspect."

A chill rippled up Angela's back, making her shiver. She stared at the mug shots of the parents, grim and haunted, their eyes bloodshot and dead like zombies. All looking exactly like Margaret had when they spoke in her cell—as if their souls had been taken from them and they were left in empty carcasses of lifeless flesh. These weren't murderers. They were victims.

"And in court, what did they say?"

"They refused to elaborate. Only that they were sorry. They never meant for their daughters to come to any harm."

"And what about between deaths? Who lived there?"

"I checked police records last night. Young couples who moved in then left a few years later. Single guys. No one that had any kids before you ask. I thought the same thing."

"So let me get this straight; over the course of thirty-odd years, five couples killed their children in the same house. Now it's six. You mentioned Amityville —why are people still moving into that house? Why aren't there morbid tours of the place going on? Why is this not common knowledge? We're police officers—no one thought to tell us about this last night? It's like it's some dirty, nasty secret or something."

"I thought the exact same thing. I don't know. To be honest, it's fucking creepy as hell. If I was a neighbour, I would have burned the place down years ago."

She thought of the way the house looked; rundown, abandoned, neglected. As if it carried the weight of all that sorrow and death in its foundations, creeping up through the walls like weeds, suffocating the life out of the place.

"Who investigated each case?"

Doug flicked through the files again. "A Detective Chris Miles. Went to every scene. I'm guessing he's retired now. Why? What are you thinking?"

"I'm thinking this is more than coincidence. I'm thinking why has it only happened to families with one daughter? Why didn't they kill each other if there was some...I dunno, weird vibe about the place? I'm also thinking I want to speak to the other parents that killed their kids. You coming?"

Doug looked up startled. "What, now?"

"Why not? My daughter's at school all day, and tomorrow we're on the early shift. Might as well make use of the day, or you got better things to do?"

"Better things to do than going to prison to visit child killers? Of course, it was my plan from the moment I woke up."

"Who said anything about prison? I want to go to Northgate."

# Six

Angela stopped outside Northgate Hospital for the Criminally Insane and sat there staring at the dark, gloomy building. Every time she passed this place, surrounded by trees as if planted there on purpose to hide it from the rest of the world, it sent shivers down her spine. She'd heard about it, of course; everyone in the surrounding villages and towns knew of its existence. Like a particularly deadly virus or legend that refused to die.

Even veteran officers talked about the place in hushed tones, as though it might be listening, ready to ensnare them in its skeletal fingers and drag them screaming towards its electrified gates, and once inside...

There was a detective who was a legend in Bradwell, Jim Morfield, who had single-handedly arrested some of the most vile psychopaths in the area—Saggerbob, Rickie Ashton. He had ended up behind the walls of the other residential hospital, for the Mentally Impaired, just before the invasion occurred. Even though the man was practically revered in this village, no one wanted to end up like him. The pay and the stress weren't worth it.

She had never met him, but she wondered as she waited for the gates to open what he would have made of the current case. Would he have made the connection straight away? How would he have reacted to what they had just discovered? Was there some sick, tortured soul out there making these poor people commit these crimes? If anyone could find the perpetrator it was Morfield. For now, though, it was on her and Doug.

The huge gate slid open like the mouth of a prehistoric monster, revealing the putrid bowels of its insides. A guard appeared around the side of the car, motioning for her to lower the window.

"IDs," he demanded, not a show of emotion on his face. Angela and Doug showed him their badges and ID cards, which he took away to a small cubicle beside the gate while he verified their details. There was a gun in his holster— one of the very few in the country allowed to carry weapons—and she had no doubt he would use it if necessary at the slightest indication of danger. No one got in or out of Northgate without going through a strict process of identification. Lessons had been learned here, painfully.

He returned their badges and IDs, asked them to remove all metallic items, and had them put them in a plastic tray. They did so, then he told them where to park and that upon doing so were to hand him the car keys as well. They complied.

It was a short path to the entrance, among trees that had lost their leaves with winter closing in, and the branches hung in the air like skeletal arms reaching out for them. To Angela it felt like walking down the path to Hell. She glanced at Doug, who presented a sombre expression, a hint of a grimace on his pale face. He knew the stories, too.

They reached the entrance and another guard pressed a button on the wall, allowing the double doors to slide open. They passed through a metal detector and entered the reception area, a woman busy typing away at her desk while doctors and orderlies wandered around.

"Sign in, please," said the guard.

The receptionist gave them a form to fill in and returned to her work. It was surprisingly warm and clean in here. From the outside, she had the impression it would be like the old asylums she'd read about in books, where mad and delirious men and women wandered aimlessly down the corridors, spiders and cockroaches accompanying them, the place smelling of death and decay, the inmates still subjected to lobotomies and electric shock treatments. But here, right now, it might have been a perfectly normal hospital like any other.

Doug stood suspiciously close to her, as if he was afraid to be left alone. She smiled, despite her nerves. Doug wasn't a big guy; she was nearly as tall as he was and he looked like a scared kid in this strange place.

"Follow me, please," said the guard. He called an orderly over, a big guy who looked like he spent a lot of time in the gym, and together the four of them walked down a corridor, their footsteps echoing like distant claps of thunder.

They were being taken to visit Wanda Jefferson. She killed her daughter in 2001, the little girl only six years old, strangling her with a rope while her husband watched. She had to be constantly sedated since then, refusing to speak to lawyers, police, or the judge. During her trial when photos of the crime scene had been shown to the jury—Wanda's defence was going for an insanity plea—she became hysterical and apparently attacked her lawyer, raking her fingernails down his face, then trying to claw his eyes out. The judge interpreted this attack as being by someone completely psychotic and mentally disturbed, to the point there was a risk of reoffending. Instead of prison she was brought here for an indeterminate amount of time. Angela had decided on Wanda because she was beginning to interpret her attack in court as something else—desperation and total, utter despair at seeing photos of her beloved child for everyone to see. In the files Doug had brought with him, she had seen a photo of the girl's corpse. She looked like a doll, her eyes bulging, filled with broken blood vessels, her bloated tongue dangling from her open mouth, and a grotesquely swollen purple throat, the marks from the rope cut deep into the flesh. If anyone would want to talk and explain what really happened to someone prepared to listen, it would be Wanda.

They stopped at the bottom of the ward, cringing each time a loud thump or wail came from inside one of the cells.

"Wanda's in here. She's sedated, but protocol dictates two employees have to be in there with you. She's not usually prone to violence or aggression, but it is what it is. No chances taken with anyone," said the orderly. He slid back a small hatch in the door and peered in, then unlocked the door. He and the guard stepped in first then moved to allow Angela and Doug in.

"Wanda, you have two visitors that want to speak to you. You gonna behave?"

She was laying on her bed, wearing white pyjamas. When she sat up and turned in their direction, Angela had to bite her tongue to refrain from gasping out loud. She noticed Doug look down at the floor, trying to hide the grimace on his face. A low hiss escaped him, as though he'd just stood on something sharp.

According to the file, Wanda was now forty-six, but she looked more like eighty-six. Her long grey hair hung down her back and chest in mere wisps, like hovering plumes of smoke, bald batches on top as if she'd tried to pull it out in clumps over time. Her body was so frail Angela had to wonder if they'd been feeding her—her breasts were non-existent and her arms and hands skeletal. Her cheekbones pushed through her skin unnaturally. Wrinkles crisscrossed her face like a city roadmap. And large, purplish bags sat under her faded blue eyes like wet teabags. There was madness in those eyes, not psychotic or burning with desire or malice, but eyes that were dead and unreadable, like a shark. Absent of life and comprehension beyond the most basic of needs.

Angela composed herself quickly and forced a smile before moving slowly to sit near her in a plastic chair.

"Hi, Wanda. I'm Angela. I was hoping to ask you a few questions if you wouldn't mind."

Wanda stared back, a glistening blob of drool dangling from her quivering lip, like snot. Angela cast a quick glance at Doug, who remained with the guard and orderly. There wasn't much hope in his eyes, either—as far as they knew, Wanda had given up the ability or desire to talk. She wasn't sure how to approach the woman now she was so close; come straight out with it or lead delicately to her horrendous crime years ago?

"I know why you're here," croaked Wanda suddenly, making Angela jump. "Really? And why might that be?"

"There's been another, hasn't there? I know. There's no other reason for you to be here, except because of that house. How old was she? Young, like mine, or older—a teenager? What did they do to her? Strangle her in her sleep? Stab her? Suffocate her?"

"I, umm..." She glanced back at Doug again. He'd perked up now, rather than slouch against the wall, his eyes bright and alert. She thought of playing dumb, not knowing what Wanda was talking about, but there seemed no point.

"Yes, you're right, Wanda. There was another one in your old house. A young girl, just fourteen. How...how did you know?"

"Like I said, why else would you be here? To let me go?" She snorted, a snot bubble blowing from her nostril. It popped and clung to her upper lip, a slick, glistening trail. Wanda seemed completely unaware or just didn't care.

"We are here because we were called to the house the other night. My partner discovered there had been several more over the years, including you. I think you were all forced to do it. Terrible as it may be. I also think the same person forced you. Is that true?"

Wanda hung her head, as if in shame. A groan came from the back of her throat as she shook her head from side to side.

"It's true, isn't it, Wanda? Someone forced you to kill Sarah. It's no coincidence that so many young girls have been murdered in that house. Tell me who did it; I'll arrest them now."

Wanda emitted another croaky snort, as if her lungs were filled with water. She was silent for a while, gently rocking back and forth, moaning softly. Then she stopped, looked up at Angela, and began to cackle—a horrible, mad noise that sounded like a diseased crow. Her gentle rocking grew in intensity until Angela was worried she might fall off the bed or smash her head against the wall. Wanda's eyes were bright and burning, glistening with tears that ran down her face to join the snot running from both nostrils. She clapped her hands as if in the throes of hysteria—something unbelievably funny Angela had just said.

Angela glanced up at Doug, the orderly and the guard, unsure if this was normal behaviour. Perhaps this was typical Wanda before the onset of a violent attack, but Doug looked as confused as she felt, and the others simply stood there watching, looking bored, as if they'd seen this time and time again. They certainly weren't grabbing their truncheons or anything to restrain her with.

Wanda's moment of delirium finally slowed down as she tried to catch her breath, coming in great bursts. She ran a hand across her nostrils and wiped it on the bed. As abruptly as it had started, the rocking was over and she was both serious and shameful at the same time.

"Tell me who it is?" she echoed, imitating Angela's squeaky voice. "You think it's that simple? All those years? All those others that killed their daughters? You think it's someone who's been stalking us for thirty years?

"It doesn't matter if I tell you who made me do it, because you won't catch him! You can't."

"Why not?"

"Because he's dead!"

# Seven

"She's been in Northgate almost half of her life, Angela, being fed God-knows-what antipsychotics and stuff. Being there with all those others would be enough to drive anyone mad, regardless of whether they were or not before they went in. You saw the way she was cackling like an old hag."

Angela nodded as she drove from the hospital, wanting to think Doug was right, but not quite as eager to accept that was the case. It was totally feasible the woman had lost her sanity by now—not just because she had murdered her daughter. Angela thought she might go mad, too, if anything ever happened to Kim. But she couldn't quite shrug off the nagging doubt that clung to her like a bad smell, slowly working its way further and further inside her body and mind. Something about that house. The impossible coincidences.

"But surely there must be some truth to what she said. Maybe she meant the person who forced her to kill Sarah is dead?"

"I assume so. But honestly, I wouldn't pay too much attention to what she was saying. She is clearly mad. I feel sorry for her and something is obviously connecting all these murders, but that woman is clearly not the one who will give us the answers. We need to look deeper. I'm just as curious as you are. Tomorrow I'll speak to a colleague who's been on the force for years. If anyone knows, he will.

"But today, it's our day off. Do things. Binge Netflix, go shopping, I dunno! I for one have to go visit my mother."

They arrived at Angela's home. It was still only midday and she was hungry, but her mind wouldn't let her take the day off. It was as if something had been ignited in her head and the only way to turn it off was find the switch and do it manually. And she already had an idea where that switch might be.

"You have a good day with your mother! And thanks for coming with me. Before Kim gets home I think I'm gonna try and find out more about that house."

"Okay, whatever. But don't let work interfere with your daily routine. Learn to separate the two things or before you know it, they blur and become one. I've seen too many cops burn out before their time."

He patted her knee and climbed out. She watched him get into his own car and drive off. She sat there for a while thinking about what he had said. She thought it strange he would say such a thing. Maybe he had family who used to be cops. Whatever the case, that wasn't going to happen to her. She had Kim to think about and every second spent with her daughter was golden. She might love her job but there were priorities when it came to sharing out her love.

But right now, Kim wasn't here, which meant she had time to investigate a little further into whatever occurred at 11 Parkland Drive. She sensed enough in that house that between leaving and arriving at the station, she had stolen a spare set of keys to the property. She felt like a criminal while doing so, as if she was planning a robbery, and it sat heavy, like a large stone in her coat pocket all this time. As she stepped down the garden path to the crime scene, feeling even more like a burglar than before, casting quick glances around the road to see if anyone was watching, her heart throbbed like it was going to explode. Whenever someone walked casually past her muscles tightened as she expected them to yell at her for trespassing. But fortunately, no one did. She wasn't entirely sure if she was technically committing a crime or not; if anything, Sergeant Wilmore might want to know why she was stealing keys to a house that wasn't her case. Exactly what her superiors had planned for it, and who would be investigating, she still didn't know. Maybe they figured there was nothing to investigate—why would they?

She pulled out the key and inserted it, unsure if anyone had been over to secure the place, despite it being cordoned off. It could take months for the house to be legally habitable again, but the next priority was to avoid kids and morbid onlookers getting a free tour of the place, maybe upload a video to YouTube —*Inside the Killer House*!—or take selfies to show their friends they'd actually been inside a real house of horrors.

The door creaked open. A musty smell, of dust and cleaning products combined, was the first thing to remind her —as if she needed it—that she was technically breaking and entering. Surely the letting agent that rented out the place over the years knew about its terrible history. They must have advised potential tenants what had happened. Checked if they had kids, daughters in particular. If they hadn't, how could they live with themselves? Didn't that make them accessories? She made a mental note to visit the agency in Bradwell and ask.

Angela stepped inside, her heart a tightly squeezed, throbbing lump in her chest, and gently closed the door behind her. The feelings she had as she surveyed her surroundings were similar to walking into Northgate for the first time; as though she had just unwittingly stepped into some secret, terrible place that would leave her scarred for life, the source of future nightmares that would have her screaming into the night every time she woke. She tried to focus on the atmosphere of the house, any residual leftovers from its near and distant past. She had found from an early age she could instinctively pick up on things, as if she could reach out and grasp at certain memories and see them play out in her mind. Her grandmother had died in her sleep when Angela was around seven. When the family was at the wake, she had been struck by the certainty her grandmother was still with them, watching from afar. Angela had noticed a hint of a shadow moving just outside of her peripheral vision, the hairs on the back of her neck prickled and she could smell the faint aroma of her grandmother's favourite perfume. It hadn't scared her at the time, more fascinated her, because she knew she loved her very much and would never do anything to frighten her. Later that night, she had told her mother, who had smiled and said she had noticed the same thing. Nothing to worry about.

She wasn't getting that feeling now, though—the house might as well have been empty forever. Her nerves were stretched taut around her muscles, like elastic bands stretched to breaking point. She had the sense *something* might happen any second, an invisible hand reaching out and throwing her across the room. She had never felt so tense, even when sent to a potentially violent call when in uniform. At least then she had a reasonable idea of what to expect, but here? Nothing.

She wandered the various rooms downstairs, absently glancing at framed photos on the walls—the Tennants with their daughter, smiling and happy, having won some award at school and beaming proudly. It seemed a travesty, an injustice, to be looking at them and sharing this memory. It was as if they had been left there as a grim reminder of what this house was all about—*Tread Carefully. Danger! Enter at your own peril*. She wondered what the remaining family members would say and do when they came to rifle through the Tennant's belongings —take it with them, or sell it, not wanting anything more to do with what had occurred.

Seeing and sensing nothing unusual, she made her way upstairs, entering the girl's bedroom. Posters of actors and singers hung on the walls, a laptop on her writing desk, her bed unmade. She wondered what secrets the laptop held. Did they contain details of her parent's treatment of her? Had they abused her in some way and something happened that caused them to snap and kill her? Maybe it was all coincidence.

"Bullshit," she muttered.

She invariably thought of Kim again, how similar both bedrooms were. A tear dribbled down her cheek as her hand stroked the blanket. She wondered if she should take the laptop with her, try and unearth secrets and perhaps the mysteries of this house, but then someone would notice it was missing and it wouldn't take long for them to come looking for her.

Instead, not wanting to linger any further, she turned to head back downstairs. She went to open the door, sure she had left it open, when there was a rustle behind her. She spun around. Nothing moved, nothing was out of place. Maybe it was the wind rustling the curtains through the slightly ajar window. The posters on the walls rippled as if to confirm her thoughts. Angela wiped her eyes and turned again to leave. The door was wide open and she just had time to see a shadow dash past towards the stairs.

"Hey!" she called and rushed outside. At the bottom of the stairs, the shadow ran past towards the kitchen at the back of the house.

"Hey, I'm a police officer. Stop!"

She sprinted down the stairs, not giving a thought to the fact that she was trespassing too, and ran after the intruder. Kids, she guessed. Probably saw her enter and followed, curious. Yet when she reached the kitchen, there was no one there. It was impossible for the person to have hidden. They would have to run past her to get to the front door. She checked the back door —locked.

"Hello? Who is in here? I'm a police officer. You're not allowed to be here. I suggest you come out now."

A creaking came from along the hallway. She looked and was shocked to see the basement door slowly swing back on hinges that creaked like wailing souls. It was impossible for anyone to have been hiding in the hallway then make a sudden dash down to the basement. And besides, if anyone ran down there, they were trapped. She doubted whether to go after them or not. Maybe it was a trick. She cursed herself for not bringing a weapon of some kind. At home she had several cans of Mace she had acquired from a questionable source which she used for work; she felt stupid now for not bringing some with her. Here, breaking into the scene of a crime known for its notorious past. There could have been drug addicts and homeless folks looking for somewhere safe to hide for a while. Doug would have called her stupid and naïve. She was a cop, for Christ's sake.

She thought she heard something down there, more rustling or whispering. Goosebumps broke out on her arms. Icy fingers squeezed her heart again as doubt gripped her—stay and see who is down there or get the hell out? But her natural instinct for investigation that was partly responsible for her becoming a cop refused to allow any thoughts of running. She took a step closer, now directly in front of the small door, and peered in. It was so dark down there it was like looking into the gaping mouth of a giant beast.

She fumbled around for a light switch, not remembering where it was. Somewhere on the wall, but in her growing anxiety she couldn't find it. She had an image of being pushed down the steps from behind and crashing down to the concrete floor below, then being enveloped in multiple clammy hands raking at her skin and flesh, low, guttural moans of delight at another fresh kill. Why this image came to her she didn't know, but she was aware of the sensation of being watched again. That if she found and turned on the light, dozens of glowing eyes would be staring up at her—the eyes of all those killed in this house now seeking absolution and revenge.

Between gasps of desperation she found the switch, tensing, preparing for the worst, but all she saw was a basement full of junk with a dark red stain in the middle of the floor.

"Fuck," she gasped, breathing heavily, clinging onto the banister for dear life.

*What the hell is wrong with me?* she wondered. She had been so convinced something was waiting for her down there, for a second she thought she had seen it, but instead of a decomposing, zombie-like body it was a stain no one had cleaned yet. But the sense of being watched remained.

She took a quick look behind her, just in case, and slowly descended the stairs. Why she was coming down here she didn't know—her brain was telling her to get the hell out and not return, but something else she couldn't quite comprehend or answer told her to continue. Maybe it was to reassure herself that the shadow she had seen earlier had been a figment of an overactive imagination—the one who kept thinking about Kim the dead girl and the inevitable question of what if?

When she reached the bottom she glanced around the dusty room, not knowing what she was looking for but conscious that the hairs on the back of her neck had risen to attention once more, that she was constantly rubbing the back of her head as if something—eyes—were burning into it. She forced her breathing to slow down—long, deep breaths—to convince her muddled brain she was frightening herself at the impossibilities of what could have occurred in this house. But the sensation she'd had so many times before that had partly caused Terry to pack up and leave were still there.

When she thought she might have regained some semblance of control over her faculties, she wandered around the small area checking that no one was hiding and careful not to step in the dried pool. Her body was still tingling with inexplicable sensations, alien thoughts in her head. She thought she could almost hear the poor girl screaming at her parents for mercy. It seemed to echo from a distance, like someone calling from far away across a mountainous valley.

Her body stiffened. She recognised that voice, it was one she knew above all others. It was calling to her, begging for help. The air in the basement grew thick, like passing through a heavy fog. She coughed and spluttered as her lungs struggled to take in air. The room darkened, like a shadow had fallen over the light bulb swinging above her. The yelling in her head grew louder, yet at the same time seemed to be coming from further away. She tried to push herself towards the stairs. She needed to get out of here and now, the girl needed her help, but she felt like she was pushing against a hurricane. Inadvertently, she stepped into the dark pool on the floor, a squelching sound as she pulled out her foot.

*Help me!* came the voice again. It was the voice of Kim, in terrible trouble, and she had to get to her fast. As she reached the bottom of the stairs using everything she had to push herself along, the basement door suddenly slammed shut. The light bulb exploded above her head, causing her to scream in shock and horror, freezing her in pitch black darkness.

"No!" she yelled, arms frantically swinging around for the wall and the stairs to get her out of here. Another voice growled in her head, a laughter that might have been a dozen fierce dogs barking at once. Kim screamed again, the animalistic barking turned to a high-pitched howl as Angela dragged herself up the stairs, each footstep on the wooden stairs like the thump of a bass drum. Something wet and sticky pulled at her hair, tried to grab her by the throat, to pull her back into the bowels of the room where she knew with utter certainty she would die if she didn't get out soon.

An image filled her head. A shadow, tall and dark, looming over her daughter, something in the shadow's hand gleaming as it was held high, poised for action. Using all her remaining strength, gritting her teeth, she reached the top of the stairs and fumbled wildly for the door handle. A sharp pain bolted through her hand, and she knew she had broken a fingernail in her struggle. She found the handle, yelped in relief and gripped it with both hands. What she suspected would happen, yet prayed it wouldn't, did—the door wouldn't open. Angela screamed in despair and desperation for the door to open, for someone to help her, that her daughter was being attacked just like the Tennant's daughter. The shadow in the image turned to face her, two flickering orbs of fire in its eyes and somehow, despite her frenzy and panic to open the door, she recognised them. She'd seen those terrible, gleaming eyes before in another realm, another reality.

From somewhere outside the basement, she heard the hoarse chuckling of a thousand demons taunting her, preparing to add yet another victim to their vast list. Angela pushed and pulled and kicked and punched the door, her throat hoarse and burning with screams that never stopped coming. But then, by pure luck it seemed, the door burst open and she fell into the hallway.

And everything was silent.

The image in her head abruptly disappeared. The corrupted howls of laughter around the house stopped as she lay crumpled on the floor, gasps of horror and relief coming in rapid succession. A part of her knew she had just suffered a hallucination, a panic attack, but even so she grabbed her phone to call Kim. She needed the confirmation. She realised Kim would still be at school—what would she say to the headmaster?

*Please check on Kim Harford. I think someone was about to stab her to death.*

She put the phone back in her pocket, forcing the deep breaths again, waiting for her whole body to stop shaking before she risked standing up. *What exactly just happened here?*

she asked herself. She replayed everything in her mind again, from seeing the shadow upstairs, the basement door being open, then that overwhelming sensation of suffocating down there when the door slammed shut. Angela was a police officer, trained to deal with events, evidence, something tangible she could work with. If some desperate person recounted to her what she had just experienced, she would have suggested a vivid imagination or panic attack.

Was that what just happened? She simply panicked when the image of Kim screaming for help entered her mind?

It was, wasn't it?

A rogue chuckle escaped from her lips. She thought of what Doug would say if she told him. He'd laugh at her and call her irresponsible—that's how the public acted, not those meant to protect and serve them.

*Fuck. Get it together, Angela, for Christ's sake.*

She pushed herself to her feet, telling herself she was being hyperactive with thoughts and ideas as she headed towards the front door, then abruptly stopped. From somewhere upstairs came the sound of something being dragged along the floor, a loud thump, then a gruff laughter that might have belonged to the devil himself. Angela bolted out the door, not even bothering to lock it behind her.

# Eight

"What's wrong? You look like you didn't sleep well last night. Hell, you look a bit like those dope heads we busted the other night. You been stealing the contraband, smoking it yourself?" Doug chuckled as he drank his takeaway coffee.

"Haha. Very funny. You don't look so hot yourself. Ever thought about shaving before going to work or is this the new you?"

"I woke up late. What's your excuse?"

Angela's excuse was that she hardly slept last night, so yeah, her eyes were bloodshot and she hadn't been in the mood to put much makeup on today. She had noticed the casual glances when she arrived at the station earlier but ignored them. She hadn't been in the mood for her fellow colleagues' jokes, either.

She had spent the better part of the evening staring absently at the TV after constantly asking Kim if she was okay, if she had a good day at school, and if anything happened. The look on Kim's face suggested she wasn't sure what her mother was talking about. After Kim had gone to bed, Angela had considered doing the same, knowing she was on the morning shift the next day, but it had been impossible to sleep. Her mind kept returning to that malevolent laughter that had caused her to run from the house like a terrified little girl. She had spent almost an hour sitting outside Parkland Drive this morning, building up the courage to go and lock the door. She had been thinking about that image, the shadow with demonic, fiery eyes holding a knife over her daughter's screaming body. The way she knew, without a shadow of a doubt, that there had been something in that house with her—it wasn't the product of an overworked imagination, after all. She had finally tried to close her eyes and sleep after drinking half a bottle of wine, and all she could see were the bodies of those dead girls in the basement reaching out for her with skeletal fingers. In the end, she got up and drank the rest of the bottle.

She couldn't tell Doug that. The pragmatic guy who believed that when you died you stayed dead. The only place you went afterwards was in the mouths of bugs and worms. Who scoffed when he heard colleagues talk of superstitious folk who reported hearing strange noises coming from abandoned buildings. "Won't catch me wasting my time on those calls," he often joked. And who would certainly, most definitely, scoff at her suggestion that she had seen and heard something in the Tennant's home. After he had laughed for a while, he might suggest she take some time off, insist she never returned to that house again—possibly even hint at informing Sergeant Wilmore of her actions—then with a serious face tell her he was worried.

But she wanted to tell him. Everything that had happened she wanted to tell him—or at least someone. For now, though, it was enough that they patrol the streets of Bradwell, looking for the usual petty criminals, while she considered other options. Like the history of that house for starters.

"I have a teenage daughter," she said in response to his original question. "Some day you might learn what it is to have to get up early, get *her* up early and ready for school."

"Not a hope in hell. I'm more than happy as I am. My ex wanted kids—that's part of the reason she left—I'm just not a kid person. No offence to Kim, by the way. She's a great kid. Might make a great Chief Inspector one day."

"Yeah, right. She so much as sees a drop of blood and she goes hysterical. My daughter is not cut out to be an officer. Talking of which, did you manage to speak to your friend? About the Tennant house?"

Doug's smile faded, replaced by the look he used when apprehending young kids for stealing or smoking dope. "I did. He was on the force when the murders started happening. Problem is, there was another killer stalking the village around the same time. Four young girls were killed, all with the same MO; sexually molested, then strangled with their own underwear or stabbed. The detective in charge of the investigation was a Detective Chris Miles, now retired, of course. He was also called in when the murders started happening in that house.

"Of course, with the parents confessing to having murdered their daughters, nothing else was done about it. Why would they? They had the bodies and the confessions, so at the time my colleague and the others put it down to the house being... not so much cursed because that would imply haunted, but just *wrong*. Of course, they were more interested in finding the serial killer. Who, by the way, was never caught, and is suspected of possibly killing three more."

Angela's eyes widened. This was impossible. In this same shitty little village not only were young girls disappearing and being murdered, around the same time, a certain house was connected to the exact same thing. Yet another coincidence.

"But I don't get it," she said slowly. "This Detective Miles. He was in charge of the task force searching for the serial killer, but was also lead investigator into the murders on Parkland Drive? So what, he was the only detective they had back then?"

"The task force was formed of eleven officers working round the clock looking for the killer. My friend said there was the possibility of a connection between the serial killer and the murders in that house, so Miles was the leading detective there, as well. They found nothing concrete connecting the two. Maybe the killer lived nearby or had some connection to that house—the similarities didn't go unnoticed—but eventually they just gave up on it."

"But as the years went by and more girls died in that particular house, no one thought it was a little more than just weird or coincidental?"

Doug shrugged his shoulders. "Like he said, they were busy with the serial killer. The last known victim was found over ten years ago. The killer just suddenly stopped. They suspect he died or moved away."

Angela shivered. She vaguely recalled reading the newspapers and seeing on television talk of a child killer on the loose, but she had her own issues at the time. That was not the kind of thing she wanted to hear about. It was around the time Jimmy died, and the last thing she needed was to read or hear about other kids being killed too. She did recall her mother warning her that after school she was to come straight home, not speak to strangers, the usual stuff, but she hadn't much choice in the matter anyway—Jimmy was her responsibility.

The killings were connected. After what she had seen and heard the day before, nothing could convince her otherwise. The question was what could she do about it?

"And the homicides in that house continue to this day. As though the place was indeed cursed. I don't care what the others say, that house is cursed, Doug. And there's a reason for it. The only time someone is murdered is when a family with one daughter live there. This Miles never thought that strange?"

Doug sighed. "Angela, insinuating a house is cursed is suggesting it is haunted by ghosts or demons or something. Like the Bermuda Triangle. It's just a sad and bizarre series of events occurring in the same place. Coincidence, nothing else. Events occur in the Bermuda Triangle because some weird magnetic shit in the earth occasionally affects planes and boats. Same sort of aberration with that house. I mean, you saw what state the outside of the place is in. Not surprising, really. Enough to drive anyone mad."

"So why doesn't anyone paint it? The letting agent should be responsible for maintenance. Why haven't they done it for so long?"

"I don't know. Ask them."

"I intend to."

Doug finished his coffee, then turned and stared at Angela as though she had said something utterly mad. "This thing has really got to you, hasn't it?"

"Yes, it has." Was this the moment? Time to tell Doug what happened yesterday? After his spiel about Bermuda and curses, she thought it might be a waste of time. Maybe it was better to go it alone with this one.

"I want to speak to this Miles, too. And read the case files again."

"Shit, you really are the budding cold case investigator, aren't you? Busting kids on dope or stealing bottles of booze too boring for you now?"

"Hardly what I signed up for, Doug. What about you? You happy to spend the next thirty years of your life walking up and down streets attending accidents, petty domestics, and kids stuff?"

He shrugged again. "Pays the bills, don't it? And keeps me from worrying about England's version of Amityville and risking getting into trouble with the Sarge in the process."

"I can live with that. And if you're so happy doing this, you can start now. Look, those two kids over there by the corner. One of them is holding something in his hand and I bet it ain't sweets they're sharing. Off you go."

Doug groaned and stepped out of the car. She followed him shortly afterwards knowing the kids would run as soon as they saw them approach. Angela wasn't in the mood for running today—she had a headache that was threatening to make her skull explode.

# Nine

"If you don't get your skinny little arse here in the next five minutes, you'll be grounded for the next year. Where the hell are you?"

Joe Glazer threw his phone on the sofa in anger. It fell on the floor and cracked. Right now, he didn't care. All that mattered was where the hell his daughter Suzy was. She should have been home an hour ago. It was the fifth time he'd phoned in less than an hour and every time all he got was her voicemail. When she walked through that door, it was going to take all his willpower not to slap her face, despite being a teenager. Just for that fact alone he felt like slapping her. She should know better than to do this to him. It had never happened before, so why now? Especially now. He had drummed into her time and time again that he didn't mind her going to friends' houses, staying a little later at weekends when she didn't have school, but she was to always, always, phone to let him know where she was, and more importantly, never come home late. If she was ever stuck she was to phone him and he would come and pick her up.

So where the fuck was she?

Joe swore out loud again and filled his glass with a healthy shot of Macallan's. He needed it. Such were his nerves he almost had to hold the glass with both hands. It wasn't just anger that tore at his heart and caused his muscles to clench tightly and ache. Disappointment because she had never done this before. She knew how much her father needed her, depended on her since her mother—his wife, Jane—had died of cancer the year before. So it was more an amalgamation of emotions coursing through his blood. And the predominant, overriding emotion he was feeling right now was fear. Fear that was more than justified.

There was a serial killer terrorising Bradwell—a killer of teenage girls just like his daughter.

So far, two girls had been found near Fritton Woods, just two miles from Bradwell. Two that they knew about and another reported missing. Two innocent young girls found semi-naked, brutalised and strangled to death. But, terrible as it was— if he was the one to catch the killer, he would personally cut the guy's balls off and ram them down his throat—these things happened to others. They were things you only saw on the news, shook your head at, perhaps offered a few silent thoughts for the families, then thanked God it wasn't one of yours and carried on with life. But right now, that wasn't the case. This time, the dreaded, horrific image every parent tried to suppress in the deepest part of their subconscious was slowly but surely creeping back out like some hideous predator. The image of seeing his daughter's photo on the Six O'Clock News, perhaps smiling energetically, as all kids of that age should, but the reporter's expression stern and serious, interviewing the investigating officer who would say that right now they had no leads and feared the worst.

His initial anger at being blatantly disobeyed was rapidly replaced by a growing pit of terror in his stomach. A dozen ideas sped through his head, yet his hopelessness only increased as he realised the answers to his questions were all negative. He should phone her friend whose birthday it was, which is why he had been slack in the first place, and see if she was still there. But he didn't have the number. That had been Jane's department — keeping a note of her friends and what they got up to. He had absolutely no idea the kind of people she hung out with, what they did, or discussed. For all he knew she had a secret boyfriend and they could be cooped up somewhere messing around with each other and she hadn't realised the time.

A sob escaped him. He had tried so hard to be there for her when her mother died. The poor girl had been obviously devastated, even though they all knew it was a matter of time, nothing else could be done to save his wife, but it hadn't taken away the sharp sting of despair when she breathed her last. He had taken time away from his building company—something he hadn't done in nearly fifteen years—to be there for her, but even then, while he tried to keep her occupied, maybe take her away for a few days, he had still spent most of his time screaming at suppliers or his foremen, speaking with his secretary at least three times a day to make sure jobs weren't cancelled, bills were paid, estimates typed up and sent out, he'd forgotten what he was doing at home in the first place— consoling his daughter.

He had assumed she wanted to spend all day alone in her bedroom, lost in her thoughts, chatting with friends. He wanted to keep himself busy, get lost in work, so he didn't have to think about the cruelties of God, fate, and everything else that spawned such upheaval in their lives. It had taken him years to turn the business into a success, the biggest construction company in the area. It almost cost him his wife before he lost her for good, so many hours a day working, forgetting they had a baby, then a toddler, then a growing girl who missed her father. Such was his determination to succeed he had become known throughout town as a person to tread carefully around, be wary of his fiery temper and lack of patience. Even the police if they stopped him for speeding were quick to tell him to slow down, be mindful of others, with their nervous, fake smile plastered to their lips rather than give him a fine. He was good friends with the Chief Inspector—having sent his boys to renovate the man's house at cost in return for a little help with loud, boisterous neighbours that moved in next door. They had soon been invited to relocate elsewhere.

And so, because of all this, even though he had been there for his daughter, he hadn't been there at all. And now, it seemed, he was paying the ultimate price—he had absolutely no one to phone who might know her whereabouts.

He picked up his phone again and stared at the screen, as if by doing so it would magically start ringing and her name would appear. Instead, he scrolled through the dozens of names and numbers, the vast majority work related, and stopped at the name of the detective leading the serial killer task force. Chris Miles, a hopeless, useless figure who couldn't find a shit in a shitstorm if his life depended on it. He didn't like the man. There was something about him that exuded an aura of mistrust and deception. When they first met at Chief Inspector Robert's birthday, he got the impression this man wasn't a detective because he wanted to serve the general public, catching killers and rapists, but simply because he enjoyed the power and authority it bestowed upon him. He was a wiry, skinny little man, with a Marine-style crew cut and piercing green eyes that could fill a lesser person wild with fear should he stumble across them. Not Joe, though—Miles addressed him as Sir, and he made damn sure it stayed that way. He wasn't intimidated by anyone.

But now, though, it seemed he would have no choice but to make the call he fervently prayed would never happen.

"Fuck," he muttered and hit call.

He held the phone to his ear while he moved over to the curtains and pulled them back. Right now, he felt like he would sell his company—fuck, give it away—if he could see his daughter walking up the garden path. But outside, nothing moved except the odd cat prowling the street.

"Miles," came a voice.

If anyone else, Miles would have screamed at the person on the other end for disturbing him at this time of night, but not Joe.

"Listen carefully. My daughter should have been home over an hour ago. She went to a friend's birthday party. Before you ask, I don't know which friend, where she lives, or her phone number. But my daughter's phone is stuck on voicemail and she isn't answering. She has never done this before. I need you out looking for her. I'd go myself, but I don't want to leave in case she does come back. Maybe she's hurt herself or something, I don't know, but I want your people out there searching."

He heard what might have been a muttered curse, muffled as if Miles had momentarily covered the microphone with his hand.

"Shit, this is bad. You sure you have no idea where she is or the friend's name and address?"

"What did I just tell you? Get your men to patrol the streets, her friend can't live far away. I dunno, track down who her friends are. But I want her found, Miles. Alive."

"Fuck. Okay, Sir. I'll get on it myself. I'll have every patrol car out looking. We'll find her, don't worry."

He hung up. *'Don't worry?'*. Yeah, fucking right. He was even more scared than when Jane had come home and said it was terminal cancer. He peered once more out the window, saw nobody, swore loudly at the empty house, then poured himself another whisky.

"Please come home, babe. I promise I'll be a better father."

He repeated this mantra over and over during the course of the night, but neither she nor anybody else answered his prayers.

When Miles offered his condolences, insisting they would catch the guy, Joe had briefly thought about hitting him next time he saw him. That was three young girls dead and another missing. If Miles hadn't caught him yet, when was he going to? From what the Chief Inspector told him, they had no clues, no evidence, no witnesses, nothing. It might as well be a ghost doing it. But now all that was irrelevant. Too late. What difference would it make if they caught him or not? The damage was done. Sure, he wanted to see him captured so other parents didn't have to go through the same torture he had, but his daughter wasn't coming back. She was buried alongside her mother in Bradwell Cemetery. Nothing mattered anymore. His company was looking to hit a million in profit for the first time —what good was that anymore? He couldn't buy his daughter back again. The only thing the money was good for now was to keep his drink cabinet well stocked. Something that was required on a daily basis now. Since hearing the grim news he hadn't gone back to work, hadn't given a shit about work. All that mattered was ensuring he woke up drunk and went to bed drunk. Eventually, even that didn't work anymore.

It seemed ironic that he had everything yet at the same time nothing. Only now when it was too late did he realise he had got his priorities so wrong. What good was money if he had no one to share it with? What was he going to do when Christmas came, their birthdays, his birthday? The same thing he'd been doing the last two months, that's what—drink himself into an oblivious state of anguish until he collapsed on the sofa.

It wasn't fair. Why him? What had he ever done to deserve this? Not just once but twice? Even that cold, heartless prick

Miles had his wife and daughter, and this guy didn't know the meaning of the word Samaritan. Why couldn't they have taken his wife and daughter instead? Anyone's except his? The world was a shithole, everything was wrong, things back to front. Would it be different in the afterlife, or was that just as fucked up and discriminatory when it came to handing out judgement and fairness? In his bitterness he decided he was going to fucking make it be. If he had to suffer so cruelly here on Earth, it was only fair everyone else suffered as well.

"Fuck it," he muttered, and went down to the basement. He had a shotgun he kept hidden that he used for both hunting and for home protection. He checked it was loaded, put the barrel under his chin and pressed the trigger.

# Ten

"Why don't we download a movie? Or even better go to the cinema? We haven't been for ages. Grab some popcorn or whatever you like, couple of Cokes, and spend some time together. I hardly ever see you anymore—we never do anything together like we used to."

Angela searched Kim's eyes for a suggestion of interest, but she found them despairingly cold. Disinterested. Not a flicker of excitement. She might as well have just asked if she'd finished her homework yet, or that maybe they work together on her maths assignments—Kim's most hated subject at school.

"Dunno, Mum. I've already got plans."

"Plans? What plans?"

"A video zoom later with Lisa and a few others. Lisa's got a new boyfriend—we wanna know what he's like."

"But you can do that anytime. You see each other every day at school. I can't remember the last time me and you did anything. And besides, aren't you all a little young to be thinking about boyfriends?"

"Lisa's fifteen, Mum," she said as if this qualified her as a legal, fully-fledged adult.

"But you can do that at school. What about me and you? We never watch movies together. I could order a pizza."

"Yeah, right. And watch when my face blows up with zits. No thanks. Anyway, I thought you were tired after being at work all day busting dopeheads?"

"That's not all I do, Kim. But that's irrelevant. I want to spend some us time."

"Maybe tomorrow."

And with that, Kim dashed upstairs to her bedroom where she wouldn't come out again unless she wanted something.

"Ugh. Kids."

She was serious about spending more time with Kim. Since going to Parkland Drive, then reading the files and what Doug had to say, she had an overwhelming maternal desire—a need—to be closer to Kim. It was as if they had been apart these last few months and their bond had broken, as though life, fate, or pure circumstance had snatched it in both hands and cut the ties between them. Kim—as she had just proven—was slowly drifting away from her, the bond stretching further and further until inevitably the day would arrive when it would snap and Kim would be gone. Not beyond repair, but not as things should be—Kim and Angela against the world. Events in that house had made her completely overprotective—that if not by her side twenty-four hours a day, something terrible might happen.

She had a tumultuous life with the loss of her father and then her brother, and Terry abandoning them. Kim was a reminder of her happiest times. Christmas when Kim still believed it imperative to leave a glass of milk and chocolate biscuits by the tree, Terry dressing as Santa Claus and giving Kim the biggest surprise of her life. Each and every birthday, the family celebrating together, summer holidays to Barcelona,

Rome, the Greek Islands and spending all day on the beach. The time Kim fell off her bike and Terry rushed her to the hospital, demanding—yelling—that she be seen immediately while she howled in pain. They were memories she wanted to share with Kim, cuddled up together, eating pizza and guiltily stuffing themselves with whatever her favourite treats happened to be at the time. They'd done it after Terry left and it had brought them closer; now, when Angela needed her most, she was drifting away.

She wasn't entirely surprised to feel her cheeks were wet when she wiped them. She turned on the TV and flicked absently through the channels to find something to take her mind off things, but it wasn't going to happen tonight. Not only was her daughter growing up and needing her less, but thoughts of Parkland Drive were occupying her mind on a constant basis. Over the last two days Angela's thoughts had been a mixture of wanting to be with Kim and wanting to delve further into whatever happened to those kids. She could barely juggle the two seemingly incompatible concepts together.

She groaned and went to fetch a glass of wine but decided to bring the whole bottle instead. She would usually turn to Netflix and watch some true crime documentary but tonight she wasn't in the mood for that, preferring something light-hearted to distract her from depressing thoughts. She found a comedy she'd seen a dozen times already, tried to watch it, but within minutes her mind had gone back to that house.

To what she had heard, that terrible, grotesque laughter that could come from nothing but something wholly evil and corrupt. Had the Tennants and the others heard the same thing? Is this what had compelled them to commit the worst possible crime? If so, where did it come from? The answers were out there somewhere, and she was determined to find them, with or without Doug's help. But now, instead of finding answers, she found her eyes getting heavy and her body sinking into a warm, bottomless ocean.

A sound, like wind howling through an open valley jerked her upright. It seemed to come from nowhere and everywhere at once; one second it seemed to come from the street outside, the next it was all around her, circling her, spinning like a vortex. The sound was familiar yet alien. Too distant, too low for her to decipher its origin. Yet the prickling hairs on her neck, her bones now composed of ice and threatening to crumble at any second, suggested she should know where it came from.

She rose from the sofa and frowned when she saw Jimmy's coat strewn over the back of a chair, the army surplus one he had been wearing that fateful day. She headed over and picked it up. In one of the pockets was his old leather wallet, given to him on his eleventh birthday. He had loved that wallet, somewhere to store the pocket money Mum gave him, and his card from Blockbusters. He said it made him feel like an adult for the first time and they all laughed.

She put it back in the coat and turned it over, then gasped and dropped it, backing away as though she'd just touched something hideous and dead. The front was covered in streaks and splatters of blood. It was still fresh—when she looked down at her hands they were smeared with crimson. There was a path of blood leading from the living room door and when she followed it, there was a long, snaking line that began at the front door which, was wide open.

In her shock at seeing Jimmy's coat after all these years, then the trail of blood, she momentarily forgot about the distant, howling sound that woke her. It was back again, causing her eardrums to vibrate, as though it was now coming from inside her head. And maybe it was because everything right now was just wrong.

Careful not to step on the glistening trail, she followed its path and saw it headed upstairs, small puddles on individual steps as though Jimmy— surely it was him—had stopped on each for a few seconds, perhaps struggling to make his way up. She heard a thump, as though something heavy had just fallen to the floor, followed by muffled screams and a bang like a door being violently slammed shut.

The wailing grew louder, as if its owner was now more desperate, sensing danger was imminent and escape was less feasible. Angela ran up the stairs two at a time, screaming for her daughter; she knew it was her making that terribly haunting, chilling noise.

"I'm coming, Kim! Hold on!"

She rushed along the landing now not caring about the splatters on the floor, skidding in her bare feet as she dashed towards Kim's room. When she reached the door, she tried to open it but couldn't. There was no lock on this door but it was stuck firmly.

"Kim! What's going on? What's wrong? Open the fucking door, I can't get in!"

She heard what she thought was barking in there and her initial thought was that a dog had somehow stumbled in off the street and was now attacking her daughter. It sounded like a whole pack of them for the deep, guttural sounds reverberated around the whole house, stinging her ears once again, making her bones rattle. She remembered the house on Parkland Drive, the sounds she heard that had caused her to run like a scared little girl. It was exactly the same noises and laughter coming from inside.

She banged harder on the door, her nerves live wires, static and sparks making her blood boil. She tried the handle again and the door swung open. As momentum projected her into the room, ready to leap on whoever was attacking Kim, she was brought to an abrupt stop, her mouth wide open ready to scream at the assailant.

She had expected some monstrous thing to be looming over

Kim, perhaps with a knife in its hand just like her previous nightmares, with that terrible barking laughter, but it wasn't. If anything, it was worse. Kim was lying on the bed, her arms raised as if to ward off any blows, whimpering and shaking her head from side to side. The person stood there covered in blood that had rapidly formed a pool on the floor wielding the long kitchen knife was no conventional monster, but Jimmy. Half his face was missing, revealing glistening brain matter and bone that looked to have been picked clean by birds or rodents, while what little flesh remained flapped against his skin, barely attached by dangling sinewy tissue. A great hole where his eye socket should have been was now a crater while the other glared back at her, a dark red colour as though the vessels had burst and blood swam in the viscous, gelatinous ball.

And yet, not even this was the cause for Angela's bladder to loosen, or for the rest of her body to tighten in horror and her heart stop as though it had impaled itself on her ribcage. The side of the face that was untouched was now her own. It grinned, as much as half a face was capable of doing.

She looked at Kim and could hear now the words she had been screaming earlier.

"No, Mum, it's me, don't do it!"

But the thing before them wasn't listening. It turned, raised the knife, and brought it down towards Kim's fragile chest, cackling that manic, laughter.

"No!" yelled Angela, and in that moment felt her body shudder. When she opened her eyes, she was sprawled on the living room floor, bathed in a cold sweat.

Panting, she scanned her surroundings, her eyes darting immediately to the chair where she'd seen Jimmy's bloodied coat, then along the floor for any tell-tale signs of blood. Everything was as it should be except for the warm, wet patch around her pyjamas. Already her head was trying to draw conclusions, make connections, yet it was as though her brain was wrapped in cotton wool, preventing any thoughts from escaping. But something was still wrong.

She realised what it was. The sound, of wind whistling through trees, howling in rage at an unforgivable landscape, was still there. She cocked her head, her heart once more as if a dagger had been driven straight through it. Yes, it was definitely coming from upstairs, not outside.

"Kim!" she gasped and rushed upstairs, not caring about having to explain the wet patch around her pyjamas. She reached Kim's bedroom door and for a second expected it to be locked, but instead she burst in, frantically looking for the impossible intruder from her dream. But Kim was alone, fast asleep. She was moaning over and over, begging her to stop, to not hurt her.

# Eleven

When Kim opened her eyes, she felt strangely tired, as if she had hardly slept. Her body ached as she stretched, making her feel as though she'd been cross country running all night instead of sleeping. She glanced at the alarm clock beside her to confirm it wasn't some ungodly hour although the sun rudely poked bright fingers at her through the curtains telling her it was definitely morning. The clock flashed 8am.

She rubbed her eyes, grabbed her phone to check any early or late night messages from friends and pushed herself up against the headboard. As she scrolled through Twitter she had to rub her eyes again; they were blurry, making it hard to read the tweets. There was a dull ache just above her left temple and her mouth was dry, as if she hadn't drank anything in days. Confused and mildly concerned, she lifted the blanket and looked underneath, guessing her period may have come early, but there was no indication it had and it didn't feel that way anyway. It wasn't just down there that ached, it was everywhere.

Her brain slowly began to wake up and distorted images flashed through her head like screenshots on an old film reel. A shadow in her room, looming over her. Something wrong with its head. Something that glimmered in the moonlight, something ominous and dangerous. And then abstract terror that her life was in danger, she was going to die horribly. As though reliving the nightmare, her intestines felt as though someone was squeezing and stretching them. It was a sense of impending doom or as if something horrific was about to happen. The closest thing it felt like was when Chris Maguire overheard Kim telling Lisa after school one day how much she was in love with him and wanted to marry him. The shame and embarrassment she had gone through, especially the next morning, when she realised she was going to have to spend all day at school pretending to ignore the sly glances and snide comments...

That was bad, but this was a whole new level. Because she remembered the face in the nightmare had been Mum's. It wouldn't be so bad—just a normal bad dream—if it wasn't for the fact that she had been acting weird lately. Unbearably so. Smothering her. As if she'd only just realised she had a daughter at all. There seemed to be a smile plastered on her face every time they bumped into each other, going out of her way to appear to be the happiest person alive just by Kim being near her. The constant questions; *how are things at school? How are you? Are you happy? Why don't we go out together? Why don't we do something together? Is everything okay?*

That was the worst one. She asked that question about five times a day, as if there should be something wrong with her and she just didn't know it yet or wouldn't admit to it. She felt like a freak with the bombardment of questions, like it was some kind of interrogation. Then there was the constant need for affection, the way her eyes lingered too long. When that happened, Kim felt like rushing to the bathroom to make sure some hideous growth hadn't suddenly sprouted on her face. Or maybe her makeup had run, causing her to look like some weird goth chick.

It made her claustrophobic and she didn't know why. Sure, they had always been close. Kim knew about her uncle, more or less, and the sense of guilt she felt and understood Mum's need to look out for her, but she had never been this smothering. Kim was fourteen, nearly fifteen, and things changed. She preferred to be with friends now, rather than at home bored and surely missing out on all the fun. Besides, Mum had decided she wanted to be a cop and knew what this would mean in regard to her working hours, the stresses of dealing with criminals and lowlifes. She was proud of her, especially after Dad left, and the shock of them being abandoned to fend for themselves like unwanted pets, yet why the sudden change now? That had happened ages ago.

But all this was in a way irrelevant regarding the nightmare last night. Because Mum acting strange worried her more. When they sat at the breakfast table in the mornings or in the evenings while having supper, she seemed strangely distant, sometimes not even aware Kim was speaking to her. Her eyes were often bloodshot and puffy, with bags underneath which made her look ten years older. Sometimes when she got up in the night to go to the toilet, she could hear her mother groaning in her sleep, restless. It wasn't the first time this happened, it was because of Uncle Jimmy, but she didn't know why she was looking so troubled and lost in her thoughts. Maybe it had something to do with what she and Doug had been discussing on the phone the other day. Something about a house and people that had died there. Mum wanted all the information he had on it and from what she could gather, it was freaking her out quite a lot.

Maybe that had caused her nightmare last night, because it had been so damn scary, so *like* Mum right now, lost and dazed, then grumpy, to the point it scared her on occasions. Only yesterday Kim had gone downstairs and watched, amazed, as her mother aimlessly put five spoons of sugar in her coffee. If Kim hadn't said anything she'd probably still be doing it. Even then she had been scared to say the wrong thing in case, well...

She shivered at the mere thought.

Kim reluctantly dragged herself out of bed, wincing at her aching muscles. A thought came from nowhere, surprising her at the abruptness of it and how abstruse it was—shocking in its suggestion. What if it hadn't been a dream at all? What if she really had been fighting off her mother?

*Bullshit*, she told herself. Her mother's strange behaviour was having an effect on her, too. Making her jumpy and edgy. Not surprising, really. She struggled to get dressed and headed downstairs, expecting to see her mother lounging at the breakfast table, and was surprised to see she wasn't. Now that she thought about it, the house was eerily silent. Was she still in bed?

That would be so unlike her, and yet, considering the last few days, that nightmare last night...A chill stole through her body, as if a cold gust of wind had suddenly blown through the kitchen. She was about to creep tentatively up the stairs to check when she saw a note on the kitchen table.

**Morning, Hon! Sorry, had to go to work early. Don't be late for school, see you when I get home. Love,**

**Mum**. xxx

That was weird, too. She never left for work without at least gently waking Kim, giving her a kiss, then telling her she had to go. Nagging her to make sure she ate breakfast, had everything she needed, and do *not* forget to lock the door behind her.

In a way, it brought a smile to her face. Three months ago—hell, three weeks ago—she would never have been left alone in the house, especially on a school day. Her grandmother would have popped by to make sure she was up and ready for school. Now, was the first step, it seemed, to being treated like an adult. Like Lisa was by her parents, allowed to stay out longer at night while Kim had to be in by ten. Eleven at the latest on Fridays and Saturdays.

Her initial unease and trepidation regarding her nightmare, mother's weird behaviour, and her aching body magically disappeared to be replaced by a sense of euphoria. Whatever was bugging Mum lately might actually work in Kim's favour. She had wanted to go to a friend's house at the weekend, knowing full well that Chris was going to be there, but if she had to be home by eleven she was going to look stupid. Tonight would be the time to ask.

Her morale raised, she grabbed the cereal from the cupboard, revelling in the fact she had the house to herself rather than being anxious about it, she sat down and started eating. She even considered not going to school, feigning sickness, just so she could take advantage of this new-found freedom. But that would mean Mum smothering her again, and no thanks. Instead, her mind wandered to whatever could be worrying her mother so much lately. From what she had gathered it sounded very interesting.

Chris was well into true crime, serial killers, and the supernatural. He once suggested last summer that they all try and get into the grounds of Northgate. See what happened, maybe they could get a glimpse of one of the inmates there staring out the window. Kim, Lisa, and the others all told him he was mad, morbid, and looking to die young. Rumours suggested that trespassers were shot first and arrested afterwards. But if Kim could find out whatever Mum was investigating, that would surely win her points with Chris. He'd be begging to come over every evening rather than go to anyone else's. Chris would be hers—he'd be *infatuated*.

She had a pretty good idea that her mother would have made notes about the case she was working on her laptop. Shortly after joining the force, she arrested a guy who was wanted for murder. She'd looked up on the internet and had proudly shown her handiwork to Kim, saving all the articles in a file titled Work Related Cases.

With an hour before she had to leave, Kim headed upstairs to Mum's bedroom. On the bedside table was the laptop. She knew the password—Kim's birthday—which, considering she was a cop, she thought it a pretty lame password to have, as though inviting people to glance through her personal stuff. She sat on the bed, opened it up, and typed in the password. Her heart a squirming thing in her chest, she opened the files and scrolled through. It didn't take long. The first thing she saw was a newspaper article and a photo of the house her mother had been talking about with Doug. '*Another Death in Cursed House*', screamed the headline. It continued, talking about a girl killed by her parents just a few days ago. Apparently, this wasn't the first time, either— it happened several times, and each time the victim's parents confessed to the murder.

So this was what Mum was so interested in. She had arrested this latest couple and must be intrigued about the coincidences. That was why she asked Doug to get the files —she wanted to delve further into the case. Kim could understand this perfectly. Just reading the article and scrolling through the past cases made her hair prickle and goosebumps push through her skin. She kept scrolling, looking for the magical word she needed to confirm what her mind was already telling her. The one that would see her rushing off to school in record-breaking time.

For some reason, though, despite it being seemingly obvious, at least to her, the various reporters failed to make the connection. Had they never seen the Amityville films? Could they not see what was happening here? It was as if no one dared to say out loud what was racing through her mind. The house was obviously, unquestionably, haunted. How else could these things happen?

Noticing it was getting late, she closed the laptop and went to get dressed, a dozen thoughts colliding together in her head. Was this why her mother was acting so strange and overprotective lately? It made sense—all those girls killed, and naturally, for any mother to contemplate the morbid situation, would feel overwhelmed about it. It explained Mum's smothering, making her feel claustrophobic, and maybe, her expressions and behaviour of being somewhere else, lost. Was Mum also considering this possibility? That she had stumbled upon an actual haunted house?

Right now, none of that mattered. What mattered was getting to school and telling Lisa, and above all Chris, about what she had discovered. She could see his face already as she gave him the news and knew what the very first words to come from him would be. *We need to check it out.*

As Kim dashed from her house, scribbling a quick text to Lisa that she had amazing news, she could already imagine Chris falling instantly in love with her, begging her to be his girlfriend. But first she'd make him wait. Wait until they'd got inside the house and see if he was as brave and tough as he made himself out to be. Suddenly, everything about Kim's life was wonderful and exciting again.

# Twelve

"Come on, Angela, you gotta stop this. What are you looking for exactly? You want to catch a serial killer who's been dormant for twenty years? Plus someone able to convince parents to murder their kids? And you think there's a connection between them? Oh, and wait. He also has to come by and check every now and then to see who has kids and who doesn't. C'mon, you're looking for answers where there aren't even any questions."

Doug sighed and sipped his steaming coffee, then shook his head.

"You told me yourself, Doug. You saw the files. Those people did not willingly kill their children. Parents do not kill their kids unless they're deranged or severely unstable. And if that was the case, they would already be in Northgate, anyway. Someone...or something made them do it, and they're all too scared to say.

"You've just reminded me to contact the letting agents. Someone must have been watching the house to see families with one daughter. Well, who would that be? The agency. Someone is responsible for letting this house and knows exactly who the tenants are. They will be able to tell us who owns it. Hell, if any staff have worked since the nineties, they could be our suspect. We should start there."

Doug stared out the window, seemingly ignoring her, watching a young couple argue outside a supermarket. It infuriated her to a degree. She knew Doug was happy just going through the motions, getting through each day without being shot or stabbed, happy to go through life without too many cares in the world. He'd told her that very thing since his girlfriend left, the life seeming to have been drained from his body, and yet, rather than patrol streets, doing practically nothing all day, here was their chance to make a name for themselves. No one else seemed to give a shit about these cases.

"Angela, we're patrol cops, not detectives. It's not our job to investigate murder, much less a serial killer cold case. If, and I repeat, if, there is a chance you are right, we would have to go to the Serious Crime Unit and tell them. They would thank us and tell us to get back out on the streets while they looked into it. And then, Sergeant Wilmore would want to know why we're not doing what we're being paid for. You wanna go through all that?"

"Yes. We could do it in our spare time, or while on patrol. As long as we're on call for any break-ins, burglaries, or the occasional domestic, the Sarge doesn't need to know. I was thinking last night, I want to speak to the very first couple to lose their daughter there. They're still alive, I checked. The father is currently at Norwich Prison."

"Jesus, Angela, you don't let up, do you? What do you think they are going to tell us after all these years? I would imagine if anything they want to try and forget what happened, if that were possible. Not have it all dragged up again. What are they gonna say now that they didn't say before?"

"Precisely for that reason. Maybe after all these years they're not scared to speak out anymore. They're in their late sixties—they've got nothing to lose."

Doug sighed. He really didn't want to do this, that was clear, but she didn't want to do this alone. She needed someone with her, should the unthinkable happen and if the accused did decide to finally speak out. She had already seen the way Kim looked at her lately, as though she were a complete stranger in their home, and she had to admit she had been zoning out quite often, losing track of time. This morning she had taken a sip of coffee and it tasted like she had put half a bag of sugar in it. Again. But she also needed Doug with her because at some point, she had an idea that the things she had seen and heard in that house would come up. She needed to speak to someone about it, and at least if Doug heard the parents describe how they were forced into killing their kids, it would make her own story more credible. Because that was what she was leaning towards—something in that house—a presence—had made them do it.

"And I suppose you want to do it today?"

"I was thinking now, actually. Norwich Prison isn't far."

"And what if we're called out or requested for backup?"

"We'll say we're in the middle of something. We got stopped while patrolling. We'll think of something. It's not as if we've got anything better to do. Or you want to sit here all day?"

"Christ. I'll do it. But only so when we're finished you understand you're looking too deeply for something that isn't there. And also, because you look like shit and you might actually get some sleep tonight."

Angela gave a little yelp of delight. On any another day she might have leaned over and kissed him.

They arrived at Norwich Prison and went through the usual routine of leaving behind all their valuables while they waited to be led to Mr Hannington. The person at the desk had been extremely surprised by the impromptu visit. When asked why this sudden need to speak to him, Angela simply said it was to do with an ongoing investigation. He looked back suspiciously but said nothing—maybe it was the fact they were in uniform that made him think she wasn't telling the whole truth.

"How has he behaved all these years?" she asked while they waited.

The guard shrugged. "A model prisoner. Wish they were all like him. Very quiet, keeps to himself. I've been here over ten years and never once heard him talk about what happened or why he did it, so don't expect to get much out of him this time around."

Angela said nothing, already feeling a knot of disappointment inside. Maybe Doug was right and they were not only wasting their time, but risking the wrath of the Sarge, as well. After a few minutes, they were called by a guard and ushered to a visitor's room where a single, elderly man sat hunched at a table. He wasn't handcuffed, which confirmed the guard's opinion of him.

They sat opposite him, a guard standing in the corner and looking bored. Mr Hannington, serving life for suffocating his thirteen-year-old daughter, looked haggard and older than his years. Heavy bags made his glazed eyes droop as though in a perpetual bout of severe depression. Wrinkles covered every inch of his pale face—so pale Angela wondered if he'd ever been let outside to exercise since he arrived. When he glanced up at them there was no smile, no expression at all, only defeat. She guessed he knew why they were here, which made her wonder why he'd agreed to see them.

"Mr Hannington, I'm Constable Angela Harford and this is Constable Doug Ramsey. We were hoping to speak to you about something that happened a long time ago. The reason you're here, in fact."

"I know what you want. No other reason for you to be here after all these years. Last time anyone came to see me was about fifteen years ago, a journalist, askin' about the house. Told him the same as I'm tellin' you, I don't know nuffin'."

"Well, I don't know if you're aware, but there was a similar incident in your old house a few days ago. Don't you think that's pretty tragic? Kind of weird as well, all those deaths in the same house, all daughters killed by their parents. You ever think about that?"

The man's eyes grew dark, as though a cloud had passed not in front of him but behind his retinas, instead. There was a hint of a quiver from his bottom lip even though she could see his jaw tighten. Her abruptness and direct comment seemed to be working.

"You don't know shit," he spat. "Not you, not anyone. I haven't even spoken to my wife in ten years, she went senile, refused to speak to anyone. We didn't deserve what happened, yet no one was willing to listen. Not that it would have mattered."

"I'm listening, Mr Hannington. Speak to me. I know you didn't do it willingly. You were forced to do it, weren't you? Just like all the others."

Watching the man's expression and body language was like watching a contortionist trying to untie themselves from a particularly complicated stunt. His jaws hinged and unhinged as if chewing on a tough piece of meat. His hands clenched and unclenched, while his body swayed from side to side, his muscles flexing, the veins in his neck taut, thick cables. He shook his head vigorously, then banged on the table, immediately drawing the guard's attention. Angela waved a dismissive hand at the guard. *It's okay. He's fine. He's about to tell us something he should have done years ago.*

She egged him along, not wanting him to clam up and close off again. It was now or never. "It's okay, Mr Hannington. We know you were not responsible. But unless you help us we can't stop it. It will continue and more innocent children will die."

"You can't stop it; don't you get it! Nothing can. Don't you think we tried? Bargaining, pleading, begging. Our daughter suffered so much before… before we stopped it from continuing. She would wake up in the middle of the night with cuts and bruises on her. At first, when her schoolteachers saw them they thought it was us. They sent investigators from social services to check up on us, speak to Jackie. But it was clear from speaking to her it wasn't us. They thought we were hurtin' her, we thought it was some arsehole at school. Some bully.

"She started having these nightmares, wakin' up in the middle of the night screamin' and screamin', saying someone was in the room with her, standin' over her. She said her wardrobe door would open on its own and something was in there, watching her, laughin' and hissin' at her. She'd go to the toilet in the middle of the night and one time she was pushed down the stairs, nearly broke her neck. That was when me and the missus talked about seeing a priest or somethin'. Or maybe —you know how teenage girls are with all those hormones and stuff—maybe she had a boyfriend and he'd…I dunno, done or said somethin' and she was being harassed or made to do things and it was playin' with her 'ead.

"But we soon discovered it weren't no kid from school, either. Weren't our daughter maybe needing a little time at Northgate. We started seeing and hearin' stuff ourselves. We'd wake up in the middle of the night and hear noises like there was someone in the room with us or outside on the landing. I'd get up to go check, thinking it was Jackie sufferin' a nightmare again, but she'd be fast asleep in bed. Yet downstairs, I'd hear the sound of furniture being moved, cupboard doors opening and closin' by themselves. I go down, nothing there. And yet, that sense of being watched, someone hidin' somewhere, ready to jump out at me…"

He closed his eyes as the memories resurfaced. The hairs on Angela's neck prickled with static. She knew exactly what he was talking about. She glanced up at Doug, whose expression was of bemusement, not sure whether to act serious or release the chuckle surely sitting behind his lips. She glared at him. *Don't you dare.*

"The bruises and cuts on Jackie got worse. One night she woke up howlin' in agony. Said her bedside lamp had risen into the air of its own accord then came crashin' down on her head. When we burst into the room there was blood everywhere, splattered on the wall behind her, running down her chest. She looked like that girl in the movie Carrie when they poured all that blood on her. She was hysterical at first, we couldn't understand what she was sayin'; it was only on the way home from the hospital after bein' stitched up she told us what had happened.

"My wife bein' all religious and that said we needed to get a priest straight away, but I told her no. If the neighbours found out, we'd have all the local journalists knockin' on our door every five minutes. I guess in hindsight I should have let her.

"My wife was at home all day while I went to work, so I missed a lot of things, but I would come home in the evenings and my wife and Jackie would be nervous wrecks. They said they'd see shadows, things moving. My wife got shoved in the back while cooking, her hand landed on the gas stove and she burnt herself. Jackie would be in her bedroom doing homework and would get suddenly thrown across the room. When she left to get her mother, the door slammed on her hand, breaking her fingers. Again, they thought it was us, more interviews, police came, but what could we say?

"That night while we were asleep, Jackie woke up screaming again. We rushed to her room and it was the same as before. Blood was pouring down her chest. Apparently, a pair of scissors launched at her on their own, then sliced her chest open just below her throat. She said she saw them hoverin' in the air after it happened, then they flew across the room and embedded themselves in one of her posters. Landed right in his throat, dead centre. We saw them when we burst in, blood running down the wall as though it was from the bloke in the picture.

"The cut wasn't that deep, so instead my wife dressed the wound and we never said a word. We told the school she had the flu so she didn't have to face awkward stares and questions, but she had homework to do—always such a good girl, wanted a career, never missed homework or anythin'—and that's when the notes started appearing. I went into her room and she was starin' up at the ceiling, like she was in a daze, her eyes rolled back so only the whites showed, and she was scribbling madly in her notebook. I called her name, shook her, but she was in a trance or somethin', and when she finished writin', I looked and it said: *Kill me. Kill me. Kill me. Kill me or he will.*

"I grabbed the book and threw it in the bin, slapped her across the face to wake her up, but instead she grabbed her pen and wrote the same thing on her writin' desk. Then, and I swear, she took that pen, held it up like a knife and stabbed herself in the hand. Then she woke up."

He was sobbing now while recounting the story. Angela was in deep shock, barely breathing. She's stopped taking notes a long time ago. She looked at Doug, who was pale, mouth wide open, eyes focused on Mr Hannington, barely breathing himself. He never even acknowledged the fact Angela was looking at him. Even the guard in the corner was listening intently, not bothering to hide the fact. Angela's heart was the only thing that seemed to be working, pounding furiously in her chest, and her skin that felt like it was alive, the skin of some reptile shedding its old coat for a new one, rippling and loose. The inmate continued.

"That was when we got locked in. We tried to phone the

police, but the phones wouldn't work. We tried to take Jackie out of the house, get her to my sister's, but whenever we opened the door to leave, these terrible cuts and slashes would appear on her body as though she had some horrible allergy against the sun or being outdoors. When a neighbour walked past, I'd try and open a window, get them to phone the police, a vicar, anyone, but it wouldn't open, either, and I couldn't break them, like they were made of bullet proof glass.

"For two days it was like this. Jackie would say stuff, but it was like someone was talkin' through her, like a ventriloquist, repeating again and again, *kill me or he will. Kill me or he will.* And as if to prove it, he'd throw her down the stairs, cut her face. It became a mantra with her, all she said during those two days was the same thing, beggin' us to kill her, make it end. Can you believe that? Imagine how me and my wife were, unable to do anything. Watching her suffer and hearin' those words from her. Kill our own daughter? I'd rather kill myself.

"But it just got more and more relentless. We'd hear screaming and howlin' during the night, coming from the basement, in the walls, all around the house. Jackie was desperate by now; she wouldn't leave her room in case it pushed her down the stairs again. She even had a knife in there with her and whenever me or my wife went to her she'd thrust it in my hands and tell me to do it. You should have seen her face covered in gashes and bruises, like she'd been attacked by rabid dogs.

"The last straw was when she tried to hang herself from the light in the ceiling. I walked in and saw her dangling there, her face blue and puffy, feet thrashing, her eyes almost jumpin' out their sockets. I cut her down and all three of us just sat there sobbing. "Do it, Dad. Just do it," she begged. And, God help me, I did. She was still barely conscious, so I lay her on the bed and covered her face with a pillow until it was over. Then I phoned the police and here I am."

The tears were running down his cheeks now, allowed to

drip onto the table unheeded. His eyes that had been cold and filled with contempt when the two officers had walked in were now empty and dead, bloodshot and glazed like a shroud had been laid over them. Angela's cheeks were also wet. When she glanced up at Doug, no expression on his face indicated whether he may believe the man or not, yet it was obvious he wasn't immune to the fact this man had murdered his own daughter—he turned away immediately after making eye contact with Angela. Even the guard was staring, at Mr Hannington, mouth wide open, like he'd just been privy to top secret information no one else knew about.

There was not a single doubt in Angela's mind that this whole story was true, not a single embellishment on the prisoner's behalf. Both he and his wife had been driven to do the unthinkable, the one thing no parent could ever even bear to contemplate. And he was not the only one guilty of such a tragic, terrible event. This man had lived with the burden of what he had done for nearly thirty years, refusing to tell anyone his story for fear of ridicule or being accused of absolving himself of blame. How were the Tennants feeling right now? They had killed their daughter less than a week ago. Were they going to suffer in silence like this man and the others for the rest of their lives? If the answer was yes, what could she possibly do to ease that burden, make everyone understand that they had been forced to do what they did?

"So, what do you think? I should be locked up in Northgate instead? Have lobotomies and shit, see what's wrong with me? Or you two just gonna have a good laugh when you get outta here? It's alright, you don't have to pretend to be all solemn and all that. I know what you're thinking."

Doug's expression never changed, but he seemed reluctant to look the man in the eyes. Angela couldn't take her eyes off him, as if searching in his very soul for more answers to the million questions she still had.

"I believe you," she whispered, hardly daring to say the words herself, yet at the same time believing them wholeheartedly. She shivered, recalling that chilling laughter in the house, the slamming of the basement door, trapping her down there.

"I believe you and somehow I will prove what you just told us is true."

The man scoffed. "Bit late for that, isn't it? You think they're gonna let me outta here someday? Whether I'm guilty or not doesn't change a thing, don't you get it? How can I walk outside, live among people again, knowing what I did? I would have committed suicide years ago if they'd let me. The damage is already done."

He was right, of course, but that didn't mean she couldn't stop it happening to others. How long before the letting agents started advertising it again, not wanting to lose any income?

"It might be too late for you, Mr Hannington, but maybe not for others. Thank you for talking to us."

She stood and did something that would have made her physically sick just a week ago. She leaned over and kissed his cheek before leaving.

They were silent until they returned to the patrol car. In the hour or so they had been with the prisoner, dispatch hadn't contacted them once, so she decided to return to Bradwell and drive past the house on their way. It was Doug who spoke first.

"You really believed him, didn't you? I must admit, he almost had me convinced, too, but you understand what he was implying, don't you? Without coming out and saying it? He was implying a ghost made him kill his kid."

"I know what he said, Doug, and yes, I do believe him. The other day, I..."

Should she tell him? Would it make any difference? Probably not. He would think she was being easily led, caught up in the kind of grief only a parent could relate to. No, let him think what he wanted. She'd wait until she had more evidence to corroborate what the man had just said and present it to him. Because her mind—however much she couldn't quite believe it, herself—was already thinking of going back inside. She had a hunch, an intuition, that if she did, the presence would reveal itself to her again and this time whatever made it act in such a way. Surely there had to be a reason, some kind of grudge against parents and young girls in particular.

"I think there is something, not necessarily a ghost or demon or whatever you want to call it, but something is making those people kill their children and I want to know what it is."

"Ugh. You really did fall for it. Earlier on you suspected someone from the agency. Have you given up on that theory before you've even looked into it? Because that seems the most likely scenario to me. If you're right about it being the same person. Shit, maybe he's even the serial killer they never caught."

"I will look into it. I'll come up with something, some reason to question them."

"Uff, if the Sarge finds out..."

"What? Gonna tell him, are you?"

"I may not necessarily agree with your conclusions, but that doesn't mean I'm going to tell anyone. I get a feeling this is more than just a maternal thing, your feelings and natural protection of Kim."

"You're right. It's not. But thanks. I won't get you involved or ask you to do anything that might put your job in jeopardy."

Doug grunted and turned to look out the window. Angela carried on driving. They reached the turn for Parkland Drive. Rather than continue, she felt compelled to drive down for another look. She didn't know why, but she had learned over the years to trust these little nudges from afar.

"Where you going?" asked Doug.

"Just wanted a quick look. Make sure there are no loiterers or kids messing about," she lied.

She drove past slowly, scanning the windows, searching for anything she didn't quite comprehend, reached the bottom, and turned around. The cul-de-sac, considering what had just happened, was back to its mundane routine, which she found strange. She expected to see journalists knocking on neighbours' doors, people perhaps on the opposite side of the road, pointing and talking in hushed whispers, taking photos to upload on social media sites. But people walked past as if nothing had ever happened; just a perfectly normal house that was showing the signs of neglect. A young teenager walked past, kicking a football. It bounced and rebounded off the wall, falling into the overgrown garden. Angela stopped and rolled down her window to tell him not to go in, stay the hell out, but the kid was too fast. He jumped over the wall, grabbed his football and climbed back over again. For one terrible second, Angela had been convinced that something bad was going to happen; that the door would suddenly swing open and two monstrous, hairy arms would reach out and drag the boy in screaming, or that he would be grabbed by invisible hands or some unseen force and hoisted through the window, never to be seen again. But nothing happened. The kid continued his journey, not once looking worried or scared about having been so near the accursed house. Angela was mildly shocked.

"What was that all about?" asked Doug, looking bored.

"Nothing. Just wondered what the kid was doing." She rolled her window up and made to drive off when she glanced up at one of the bedroom windows. One of the curtains was moving slightly, as if someone had just pulled it aside. She stopped again, her heart suddenly awoken once more from its lethargy. Then a shadow appeared in the corner of the window, growing larger, as if a cloud was moving across the glass. The shadow took on a more human form, the clear rounded shape of a head, shoulders, a chest. It grew right before her, as if materialising out of thin air, until two pinpricks of silvery light appeared, blinking rapidly. Its features became more distinct—a mop of curly, black hair; an old army surplus jacket that had a disturbing dark patch in the centre. One of the pinpricks grew bigger than the other, like a star closer to the Earth than the other. Something dark dribbled down one side of the figure's pale face before it suddenly disintegrated, so now the head resembled a punctured football or a melon that had been crushed on one side, and that was when Angela gasped. She almost screamed when an arm rose and pointed at her, something long and gleaming in its bony, withered hand.

She turned to Doug, who was looking in the opposite direction, needing him to see what she was seeing, her brother, pointing at her with accusatory fingers and a face that was missing half its flesh and bone, yet as soon as she tugged at his sleeve, then looked back up at the window, the figure had gone.

"What? Now what?"

But Angela couldn't speak. Her vocal chords had frozen, her throat was constricted, making it difficult to breathe, her heart slamming itself against her ribcage.

"For Christ's sake, Angela, what's wrong? You look like you just saw a ghost."

But she said nothing. Because she had just seen a ghost, and not just any ghost, so how could she tell him that? It was only after ten minutes of insisting that she finally snapped. "Just shut the fuck up, will you?"

# Thirteen

It had been her first serious argument with Doug after telling him to shut up, as if they were married and cracks were starting to appear in their relationship. She'd never even swore at Terry when they were married, let alone a colleague. But the way he seemed to take everything with relative disinterest, rarely getting stressed or nervous, refusing to believe anything that couldn't be proven in a court of law like a typical cop. Unless he could see it in an evidence bag or written down on a confession sheet, as far as he was concerned, it hadn't happened or simply didn't exist. So, the smirk on his face after seeing her brother in the window had been a catalyst. Lashing out at him with a need to vent her terror at something or someone. Just who the hell did he think he was to smirk at her that way? It had been her brother up there, threatening her, taunting her, not just a figment of her overactive imagination. A brother who was dead because of her and who it seemed had decided to return to remind her of the fact. At just the right time, when she was at her most vulnerable.

After telling him to shut up, he had turned defensive, almost aggressive, if it was at all possible for such a passive figure. He called her obsessed, that her shock at what she had seen and heard from the Tennants and the subsequent visits to parents was getting to her. Yes, he understood that her brother had died, that her husband had left her and Kim, and that her maternal feelings were stronger than ever, but even so, her behaviour wasn't normal. She was a cop and supposed to keep her feelings at home or at the bar after work. Let the detectives do their job; you do yours. She had been close, very close, to blurting out that she had seen her dead brother in the Tennant's window but bit her tongue and just managed to avoid doing so. In hindsight, she was glad she kept quiet. That would have raised immediate red flags with Doug, and she still wasn't entirely sure she could trust him to keep his mouth shut. Instead, she had told him he was a heartless zombie like the psychopaths who lacked any form of understanding or empathy. Doug had replied that yes, he did care about others—that was why he was a cop, just like her—but he sure as hell wasn't going to lose sleep worrying about a supposedly haunted house. Go speak to the fucking letting agent instead of searching for ghosts, he spat at her.

For the rest of their shift, she had driven around Bradwell seething, wanting to respond with some hurtful or clever comeback, but she had restrained herself. The idea of telling him what she had seen in that house, so she knew damn well it to be true, was constantly on the tip of her tongue like a bad taste in her mouth. Instead, she had taken out her frustration and annoyance at every little incident they had come across; the two drivers arguing over a parking space who she had told that if they didn't shut up and clear off elsewhere, she'd arrest them for fighting; the guy who had gone through a red light who she sped after and screamed at for not obeying the traffic lights and what a public danger he was; the kid riding his pushbike on the pavement who, by the time she had finished, walked away sobbing, such had been the intensity of her verbal reprimand.

All the time, Doug had remained in the patrol car, not wanting to get involved. When their shift finished, they never even said goodbye to each other.

But that was yesterday. Today was Saturday, her day off. She had wanted to spend the day with Kim, do something fun to unwind and forget about the stress of her job, but Kim already had plans—something Angela was starting to hear far too often these days. She thought of going to visit her mother, perhaps they could go out, eat Chinese food at the new shopping centre that had recently opened, but something pushed these thoughts from her head, banishing them like a rude guest.

It was that house. This case.

It refused to budge, sitting there stubbornly at the front of her head, first in line, not allowing any other idea or thought to push past. It would have been nice to spend the day with her mother or daughter, but it would be oh so much nicer if it had been any day other than a Saturday. She would have taken up Doug's suggestion and gone to the letting agents and insist on speaking to the manager. Today would be too busy with customers, and as it was not her case she wanted to avoid being seen by anyone that could question her. The plan formed inside her head now sat there proud and determined, refusing to be denied.

*Go back there. Go back inside and see what happens. Try and make contact with whatever is haunting the place. Find out why, above all, it is so determined to make all these families suffer so cruelly.*

And it was such a good idea. Despite what happened last time she went there alone, she was confident that she could resolve this issue. Perhaps by asking the right questions, offering help to whatever roamed the empty rooms, so it didn't have to happen again. No more poor kids or parents had to suffer again. And then, of course, there was the issue with the letting agency. They would begin repossession proceedings and find new tenants as soon as they could, meaning her chances of this would very likely be gone forever. *You could rent it yourself, there's a thought*, her morbid brain told her.

"Forget it," she muttered. That house might be acting as some magnet, a black hole trying to suck her in through the front door, but there was no way she was putting her daughter at risk. She had to admit, though, that the thought had passed through her mind on several occasions. *Kim could stay at your mother's place for a while. You could live there a couple of weeks, see what happens.* Yet as much as the idea sounded tempting, she quite simply couldn't afford it.

So that left one option.

She finished her coffee and headed upstairs to get dressed. It was still only ten in the morning and Kim had already left. She had no idea what was so urgent for her to leave that early. Kim *never* got up before ten on a weekend. Part of her wished Kim would let her be more involved with whatever she had going on, like before when she confided every little secret in her; the kid at school who had a crush on her; talking about sex and how it all worked; Terry; and Jimmy...That part of her life was rapidly fading too, it seemed, lost forever. The next stage would be Kim going out with her friends and not even bothering to tell her where she was or with whom. She dreaded the moment Kim came home with a serious boyfriend to tell her she was pregnant. She prayed Kim wouldn't think about doing anything rash; at least until she had her career defined.

Again, inevitably, as she dressed, she thought once more about all those parents from 11 Parkland Drive who would never get to see their little girls grow up, never have to worry about becoming a grandparent a little too early, worrying where the hell she was at three in the morning and if she was out doing drugs. A tear dripped down her cheek. She wiped it away and tried to concentrate on the task at hand. Kim was a sensible girl, always had been, and wouldn't do anything stupid.

Before she left, she checked her laptop. She'd been collecting information about the serial killer, asking for anonymous tips on a fake Facebook account, someone might know something but not want to go to the police. Maybe it was the killer himself who was now old and carrying a great burden—maybe he'd like to confess his crimes under the safety of impunity. But there were no new messages. She found it strange, the screen displayed her last log in time as yesterday. As far as she could recall she hadn't been on her laptop at all yesterday—she'd been too busy being angry with Doug all evening and watching mindless old movies on Netflix. Maybe Doug was right; maybe she was losing her mind.

She closed her laptop, slightly disappointed no one had come forward, yet now excited and nervous about revisiting the house. She briefly considered taking a weapon, then decided against it. If whatever was haunting the place decided to acknowledge her presence, no knife or can of mace was going to help her. Angela rushed downstairs, grabbed the key to the house and left.

As always, when she approached Number 11, she did so with a feeling of apprehension, casing the place prior to breaking in. She decided to park further up the cul-de-sac for reasons she didn't quite know, which made her feel even more like a common thief. She climbed out of the car and looked up and down the street, again amazed to find life continuing as normal, as if nothing exceptional had ever occurred. On a whim, and after Doug's comments, she had browsed the internet to check out the Amityville in America. For weeks after the release of the original film and every subsequent sequel there had been morbid sightseers camped outside taking photos, a police presence required to stop anyone from breaking in, like it was home to some famous celebrity. Yet none of that was happening here—not even some enterprising journalist who might have made a few connections. The sensation that something conspired to keep the grim events in the house secret was once more reinforced.

A feeling of being watched stalked her as she walked down the garden path. Whether it was coming from inside the house, or neighbours watching from across the road, she didn't know. At any second, she expected to receive a tap on the shoulder, a *'what the hell do you want?'* to be yelled ominously into her ear. As she entered the key into the lock, she realised her muscles were tense, she was holding her breath, her ears straining for the sound of footsteps behind her. Before the key turned the door swung open and she remembered she had previously left it open in her haste to escape. Now her focus turned to what may now be in front of her, hidden behind the wooden door. A pair of arms ready to drag her inside, the door slam shut, and Angela never to be seen or heard from again. Or a face, perhaps that of her dead brother, his brains dribbling down what remained of his face, or maybe that of some hideous, spectral creature, dead for decades, yet still searching for more and more victims to add to his collection. She felt sandwiched between two horrors—one real, the other a disembodied killer from another realm.

But she couldn't stand here like this all day, so she took a deep breath and stepped inside. What flew out to assault her wasn't some phantom monstrosity, but a slight gust, riddled with dust and tainted with the musky scent of unclean air. Angela exhaled and closed the door quickly behind her.

Her senses came alive immediately as she scanned the hallway. Her eyes searched for the slightest movement or inexplicable shadow hiding in dark corners; ears straining for the creak of a stair or floorboard upstairs, that terrible wailing and laughter that had haunted her dreams since the incident in the basement; maybe some pungent, foul smell rushing to greet her, but most of all it was her brain that searched for any indication of other signs, a sixth sense telling her what was to come or what she should be wary of. Yet nothing came. To all intents and purposes, it was just another house. She glanced towards the basement door under the stairs, expecting it to slowly and eerily open of its own accord, yet it was firmly closed, no sounds coming from down there to alert her of a presence.

It was the same apprehension she felt when called to major incidents with Doug, not knowing if as soon as they knocked on the door they would be shot, stabbed, or just received with extreme resentment. The sense of the unknown, of trying to be prepared for any eventuality.

She had come here with the intention of trying to make contact with the haunted soul infecting this house like a parasite, try and get it to tell her why it needed to kill so many innocents over such a long period of time, but now she was here, sensing nothing, she felt a little silly. *Maybe Doug was right*, she told herself. *Maybe I am looking too deep.*

*No. Something made those parents murder their kids. It couldn't be the letting agent, who also happens to be a wanted serial killer, getting his kicks making them kill their children. It has been going on for over thirty years. If human, it would have left evidence, a trace.*

Unsure exactly what to do, trusting her instincts, she headed upstairs. The image of Jimmy pointing at her from the upstairs window reappeared in her head again. She had been questioning herself repeatedly as to whether she had imagined it or not, like Doug said, because she could find no connection between her brother and this house at all. But then she thought about the nightmares she had, featuring her brother as an uninvited guest, the way Kim had been screaming and that cyclopic eye of Jimmy's daring her to stop him. If there was a connection, she wasn't seeing it yet.

She hesitated before opening the bedroom door to where Jimmy had been. Would he be standing on the other side, waiting for her? The spirit in this house taunting her, with the ability to search deep into her most haunted memories. Was that part of the game, too?

She opened it. Nothing but dust attacked her, the air in the room warm and oppressive from the windows being closed for so long. Nothing had been touched since the Tennants had been arrested, except by Forensics looking for any clue as to a motive. She was about to turn and leave the room when she heard muffled sirens in the distance, what sounded like a police car rushing to a crime scene or accident. Her heart immediately ignited in her chest as was customary—it might have been her day off, but she, like all the others on the force, with the possible exception of Doug, were never able to switch off the little circuit in their brain that sparked under certain circumstances.

Angela left the room and closed the door behind her. She headed towards the next bedroom, still hearing the sirens, slightly louder now. She entered the next room and was greeted with the same musty smell of emptiness. She was very tempted to open a few windows and let some fresh air in, but this could alert some nosy neighbour and that was the last thing she wanted.

She thought of calling out to the spirit still under this roof, but the extra sense that she possessed failed to pick up the slightest sign of any foreign energy, so she abandoned the idea. This room was a spare bedroom. The bed was made, and nothing decorated the walls save the odd cheap painting here and there. She opened the wardrobe to find it completely empty, fuelling her suspicions. Somewhat lost in her thoughts, she closed it again and headed back to the landing when she realised she could still hear those sirens. She looked out the window—maybe something had happened on this street. But when she peered out from behind the curtain, there were no flashing lights, nothing. Confused, she left.

She thought about the last time she'd been here. Everything

had happened when she went to the basement, as though it was the epicentre of the tumultuous events that had occurred here; perhaps a catalyst for the entity to appear, as if drawn from its hiding place. She headed slowly down the stairs, eyes searching once more for the slightest movement, yet her ears were already occupied. The sound of sirens was even louder now, as if police cars were somehow parked in the living room. Concerned, she quickly headed there and peeked out the window, careful to ensure no one could see her. Again, nothing. The noise was loud enough it should have been right outside the house.

She closed the curtain again and tried to ascertain exactly where the sound was coming from. But as she circled the room, she realised to her dismay and shock that it seemed to be emanating from inside the house, as if someone was playing a song somewhere that consisted of nothing but police sirens. It was coming from above, to her left, right, and when she squatted and put an ear to the tiles, she could feel the floor vibrating. She recalled her thoughts about the basement and headed towards the little door under the stairs.

It was definitely louder down there. When she touched the door handle it vibrated, too. She opened it slowly, unsure what to expect, and when it was wide open, the ear-piercing sound of sirens almost deafened her. She gasped and covered her ears, even though she was used to the sound by now, because somehow this was louder and more intense than any she'd heard before—even when it was her own patrol car making the screeching rhythm.

She crept slowly down the stairs, conscious of what happened the other day, and the door slamming shut behind her, trapping her in darkness. Today she had thought to bring a small torch with her, just in case. Her head was throbbing now, in time to the pulsing noise of the sirens, but as soon as she touched the dirty floor of the basement, the sound abruptly stopped. Her ears were ringing and she briefly considered if she'd suddenly gone deaf. It was so quiet, like someone had grabbed her brain in both hands and rattled it violently. But she could still hear the sound of her own heavy breathing, her footsteps on the concrete floor. She managed to avoid the dried pool of blood that still had her sole print embedded in it.

It was clear that whatever haunted this house had caused that noise. How, she didn't know, but she was more interested in why. She walked slowly around the basement, her breathing laboured, as if she'd just been jogging and struggled to get her breath back.

"Is there anybody here?" she asked finally. "Where are you? What do you want? I came here to help."

Her ears finally stopped ringing and her brain shaking as she strained for any sound of the spectral killer. She glanced up at the basement door expecting, it to slam at any moment. The light bulb that had smashed the other day still covered the floor in dozens of tiny pieces like bone fragments. Her fingers grasped the small torch in her pocket. In her other pocket was a small penknife, nothing too big but enough to ward off any drunken idiot or someone with bad ideas. It had become a custom of hers to carry it with her everywhere, in case something happened on her day off and she needed to intervene. She pulled it out, not sure why, but the thought had suddenly popped into her head, as if it was a necessary thing to do.

Angela held it up as though about to stab someone only she could see. After a few seconds and nothing happening, she was about to put it back in her pocket when there was a sudden creak on the stairs. In her surprise she almost dropped the knife as she swung towards the sound. Another came, then another —the unmistakable sound of something coming down the steps, something heavy, that caused motes of dust to shoot up like tiny sandstorms. Her lungs tightened, the hair on the back of her neck prickled with static. Another thud came. She could visibly see the wooden step indent as the invisible weight was put upon it.

"H-hello?" she said, timidly.

A slight gust of wind blew past her face, bringing with it the tangy aroma of rotting vegetables. A tiny cloud of dust rose from the floor as the thing reached the bottom of the stairs. She was vaguely aware of some distant noise, like muffled groaning coming from all around her, just like the sirens. It was as if the house itself had suddenly woken from a long sleep and was yawning. It grew in pitch and intensity until it sounded like the foundations themselves were splitting, the house about to collapse on her at any moment.

The floor beneath her shook. She took a step back as the air in front of her eyes, directly before the stairs, shimmered, as though her eyes had blurred, impeding her vision. It was like the heat rising off tarmac on a boiling day, never quite forming into anything tangible and recognisable, but seemingly trying to. Groans echoed around the room like the wails of a thousand departed souls. The cloud-like formation swam and wavered before her, drawing closer then further away as if unsure whether to approach or not. She wasn't scared, although her heart and nerves begged to differ. Rather than scared, she was more enthralled, in awe of what she was seeing. Even though she had seen plenty of things before, like the ghost of her grandmother, and shadows across her vision, she had never seen anything like this, yet given what its owner might be, a certain sense of unease made her blood thicken in anticipation.

"Who are you? Are you making these parents kill their daughters? Why? Let me help you."

What sounded like a roar, some huge feline in great agony, shook the walls. It caused Angela to stumble backwards. An image filled her head; Jimmy brandishing a knife with most of his face a dripping mess, like a melting wax sculpture. Kim was on her knees begging him to stop, her own face slashed so the skin hung like old wallpaper.

"No!" cried Angela. "I want to help you. Tell me why. Why are you doing this? I can help."

Then, without warning, her knife flew across the room, the blade embedding itself in the plaster. The ear-splitting sound of the sirens returned, making Angela scream, barely hearing herself. When she looked up, she was shocked to see her knife was now a red colour, what appeared to be blood dripping from it, running down the wall and collecting on the floor. A word was formed that resembled something like the popular sport manufacturer, NIKES. The knife wiggled as though someone was trying to pull it free, then it shot across the room towards her, missing her face by inches before hitting the wall and landing beside her. The shimmery form was acting as though it was agitated, spinning frantically, growing large then shrinking, lights flickering inside it like stars. It came to within touching distance of her then rapidly backed away again, a distant wailing sound emanating from within its spectral shape.

It was trying to tell her something, of that she had no doubt, but what, she couldn't fathom. The knife started to spin beside her, like the effervescent form, then Angela watched in amazement as it slowly rose and hung directly in front of her face. She reached out to touch it, blood still dripping as if coming from within the knife itself. But just as her fingertip touched it, she felt a sudden jolt, like she had been hit by a live cable. She screamed and quickly pulled her finger back. The penknife continued rotating, drawing slightly closer then retreating, then after a few seconds it dropped to the floor as the sound of the siren faded away. When she looked up again, the cloud-like shape had gone.

Silence reigned in the basement. Only her breathing and the sound of her heart clashing against her ribcage suggested she wasn't deaf. Her mind reeled with a thousand thoughts and possibilities. She didn't know where to start. She was convinced she had just been witness to the entity that haunted this house, forcing its residents to commit unspeakable crimes. And yet it hadn't tried to frighten or harm her like before. She was sure it tried to show her something, give her a sign. She replayed in her head what had occurred; the deafening whine of the sirens; her penknife, which now showed nothing of the blood she'd seen moments before, launching itself at the wall, then back at her, hovering before her face like some inquisitive flying bug; Jimmy about to kill Kim. But what? None of it made any sense. Was it trying to warn her? Maybe it had been warning her to get out—that the police were not welcome here, it still had unfinished business to attend to.

She picked up the knife and scrutinised it, turning it over. It seemed the blood she had seen pouring from it had been a hallucination, after all. Her hands still shaking, she put it back in her pocket and ran a hand through her hair as she pushed herself to her feet. Whatever just happened proved at least that she wasn't mad, as Doug had said. There was no way she imagined that. As she was about to head back up the stairs, she happened to glance at the floor. The dried pool of blood was glistening as though fresh. She bent down to have a closer look and realised the footprint she had left on her last visit was not hers. This was a Nike baseball boot print clearly formed in crimson. She stared at it for a while. Was that a clue? Someone she should be looking for who wore Nikes? She had no idea so pulled out her phone that she had forgot was in her pocket and took a photo. Excitement thudded through her as she left and locked the door. What was Doug going to say if and when she told him about her ghostly encounter?

# Fourteen

Doug stirred in his bed and opened an eye. The sun was shining directly through the window, which was a good sign. It meant he didn't have to go to work, it was his day off. The only time the sun ever temporarily blinded him when in bed was when he didn't have to get up and go to work. His still-frazzled brain reminded him that today was Sunday—suspicion confirmed. He closed his eyes again, trying to tempt his brain into going back to sleep, but that was pushing it. He must have slept at least nine hours already—almost a record. For some reason, though, he didn't feel like he'd just slept nine hours. It felt like a normal waking day, still lost in the slumber brought on by lack of sleep, his body still tired and demanding more rest.

As his brain slowly geared up, he remembered why. He had had a bad dream in which he'd been attacked by some ruthless gang that was going to kick him to death for insulting their leader, Angela. She had appeared carrying a huge sword and had made him kneel, raised the sword high, ready to slice his head off. All for daring to question her beliefs, and he was sobbing, telling her he believed her, it was a monster killing those kids, a demon, and he should never have doubted her. And when the sword had been about to fall, her face had suddenly changed into a terrible, zombie-like thing with bits of flesh falling from her face like confetti. A cyclopean eye and a mouth stretched wide across her face, cracking the skin and revealing dozens of tiny, pointed teeth. He realised now he had awoken just as that sword came down to meet him while Angela cackled with delight.

"Fuck," he muttered, then the memory of arguing with her on Friday returned. *Shit, she must have really got to me with her stupid, wild ideas*, he told himself. Talk of vengeful ghosts and psychotic letting agents who might really be serial killers from over thirty years ago, having given up their morbid little hobby.

She worried him. They weren't best friends by a long stretch, but when two people are paired together at work for eight hours straight, inevitably personal issues and emotions filter through. He'd told her about his breakup and very little else because he didn't have much to offer—he was more than happy to get through each day with as little stress as possible with no great ambitions in mind. He'd often thought about joining the much busier Serious Crime Unit, rather than spend his days arresting kids and drunks, but excitement also came hand in hand with stress. And that he could do without.

Angela, meanwhile, seemed attracted to it, obsessed even, and that was what he told her on Friday which had brought a reaction from her he'd never seen before. He'd struck a nerve, it seemed. But, dammit, he was right. Yes, it was bizarre, all those kids murdered under the same roof, but to think it was the ghost of some long-dead vengeful spirit was ridiculous. Maybe she'd been watching The X-Files for too long. He would be prepared to admit that perhaps something weird was making the parents do what they did, some negative vibe in the place or something. He'd read about certain areas in the world that had an unnaturally high suicide rate, where people would go specifically to commit such an act, a forest perhaps, or a particular bridge, so that was a possibility, but enough to make people kill? Bullshit. What was happening was that someone in the area was targeting that house for whatever reason and bullying them into doing it. Maybe some freak who should be in Northgate, whose parents had previously owned the place or something. But the original detective had looked into everything and found nothing. And it was not his job or rank to undermine them.

And it wasn't Angela's, either. She was becoming grumpy, she looked like shit, snapping at him whenever he tried to bring up the subject again, risking not just her job but his as well. Going to prison and listening to that lunatic talk about being forced to kill his daughter was a ploy, nothing else. Maybe to get the chance of probation. Well, it wasn't going to work, and Angela needed to listen. Maybe it was time he had a proper chat with her, made her understand she was putting their jobs and her health on the line. He had an idea she'd been back to the house, too. The other day he'd seen her take the set of spare keys to that house. If she wasn't careful, she was going to not only lose her career, but get arrested in the process.

Begrudgingly, he threw back the blanket and climbed out of bed. He staggered downstairs, revelling as always in the peace and quiet of his home. No wife, no screaming kids, no dogs or cats demanding to be fed or walked. Just how he liked it. He did often wonder if he would enjoy it as much when he was older and retired, with no one to talk to, but there was The White Horse pub for people like that, who could happily sit and whine and moan all day to their heart's content. Maybe he'd go live in a retirement home, so he didn't have to cook or do any housework. Certain parts of his anatomy did miss female company, though, which was a problem, but being a cop had its perks—he knew where all the best prostitutes hung out. Perhaps tonight after he'd seen Angela, he'd go pick one up.

He finished his coffee, thinking about how to best handle Angela, then had a quick shower and was ready to go. As he drove off, not bothering to phone and let her know he was coming, he thought about how he might try and get her to see reason. He was more than willing to help her if necessary, but a line had to be drawn if she was trespassing on the property and carrying out her own investigation. The last thing he wanted was to see her thrown off the force.

He came to a crossroads. Angela's was to the left, but Parkland Drive was to the right, just ten minutes away. Out of curiosity, although not quite understanding why, he decided to run past the place. A quick detour down the cul-de-sac to make sure the door was secure at least then go see his partner.

He shook his head as he turned right, feeling somewhat stupid after everything he'd decided earlier. If anyone saw him driving randomly down there and it got back to the station, it might be him answering awkward questions instead. Sighing, he reached Parkland Drive and slowly drove down. When he came to the house and saw people walking past without giving it the slightest attention, he did have to agree with Angela that this in itself was weird. There should have been journalists knocking on doors and taking photos of the grim house. Kids daring each other to go and knock on the door. The local cursed, haunted house, and yet everyone ignored it as though nothing had ever happened there. When a local serial killer, Harold Saggerbob, had been caught after decapitating fourteen kids, locals and even people from across the country had camped outside the house for weeks. He wasn't sure but he thought a small group of Japanese sightseers might have flown deliberately across the world just to see it, too.

Doug drove past the house, reached the bottom of the road then turned around. He thought about parking and going to check the front door was in fact locked, but nerves got the better of him. The last thing he wanted was some irate neighbour shouting about onlookers and trespassers. But as he slowly drove past, shaking his head at the jungle that represented the garden, the flaking paint on the house, and the grimy, filthy windows, his heart suddenly jumped into his throat. He hit the brakes and looked up at what he assumed to be a bedroom window. The curtain twitched.

At first he assumed it had been a trick of the light or he'd simply imagined it, letting Angela's bizarre theories get to him, but now that he was looking up at it, he was positive he could make out the dark outline of a person standing there, just behind the thin curtain fabric.

*Angela. It's fucking Angela. She's gone and done what I knew she would. Shit, she's gonna get the both of us sacked, the stupid woman.* Now angry rather than uneasy, he turned off the engine and got out. This was going too far. If a neighbour saw her there and phoned the police she'd be arrested for trespassing and sacked. What was she going to do with Kim, then? And now, he felt compelled to go in and drag her out, thus hindering his own career.

"Fuck, Angela, what the hell are you thinking!" he spat.

He quickly looked around to ensure no one was watching then hurried down the garden path. Before he tried the door, he took a deep breath, still not believing what he was doing, or more importantly, Angela. Everything he had planned on saying to her was now going to be rammed down her throat until she listened. Fuck her pride and hurt feelings. Doug tried the door, and was not surprised to see it unlocked, and stepped in.

The first thing to hit him was the clogged air supply, thick and heavy, and smelling like an old fireplace. He imagined it like being trapped in a basement or some other enclosed space. The last time he had stepped foot in here the windows had been open and there had soon been officers running around the place —now it felt like stepping into a mausoleum. Despite his opinion on what had happened here, it still upset him to see photos of the family on the walls, a small table beside the front door with a set of keys on them, a coat cupboard filled with jackets and umbrellas. A pair of girl's Nike's sat by the door. It was as if the family had gone on holiday and he'd been asked to keep an eye on the place, feed the cat. All this stuff was junk unless a family member decided to keep or sell it. He'd heard a detective talking to family members on the phone, arranging days to come to the house and organise the funeral, but back then his mind had been on the cruel, callous parents and what they'd done.

The circumstances surrounding the events were making him uneasy, as though he really had walked into a haunted house. He felt eyes watching him from some secret, dark corner and it made him shiver with unease. He remembered what he had come here for and called to Angela to get the hell down and out of here.

"Angela! I know you're up there. Get the fuck down here now. We're leaving!" he yelled when she failed to respond to his call.

He thought he heard movement coming from upstairs, a floorboard creaking and footsteps directly above his head. He muttered another curse and headed up the stairs. Halfway up he stopped and spun around, sure there was someone watching him. It reminded him of the time he'd been called to a car park one night after someone had phoned in to say they saw a couple of drug dealers exchanging their wares. As he'd wandered around the almost pitch-black car park, he had been convinced the dealers were lying in wait for him, hiding behind cars waiting for the right moment to pounce. After five minutes he had rapidly left the scene, fearing for his safety, and that sensation was with him again.

He quickly headed upstairs.

"Angela, get the fuck out of there. I know you're there—I saw you from outside. You're gonna get us both arrested," he called. When there was still no reply, he cursed again and barged into the bedroom where he'd seen the figure.

There was no one there.

Even angrier than before, he checked behind the door, in the wardrobe, behind the curtain, even under the bed. There was no way she could have got downstairs without him seeing her, so he rushed out and threw open the doors to all the other rooms upstairs, calling her name, telling her to stop fucking about, but when he'd checked every room, under every bed, and inside every wardrobe and still hadn't found her, the first tingle of fear rippled up his spine. He questioned what he'd seen again; no, no way, he had not imagined seeing that curtain move or the figure standing there. So where the hell was she then, and why wasn't she answering him?

A sliver of an idea, one so ridiculous he banished it before it could take on a more substantial form, flashed through his mind. What if the parents they'd spoken to at Northgate and Norwich Prison had been telling the truth?

"Bullshit," he muttered.

*Where is she? Phone her, see if her phone rings. If it doesn't, you might be in trouble. She might not be the only one hallucinating lately.*

He pulled out his phone and searched through his contact list. He found her name and hit dial. His heart was thudding now, as if he was phoning his doctor to get test results back from an alarming lump he had spotted on his body. In a way praying the doctor wouldn't answer so he could continue pretending it was nothing, yet not wanting to prolong the torment either. Both possibilities had their pros and cons. Now though, he prayed she did answer, or at least he would hear her familiar ringtone playing in the house.

After a few seconds when the phone rang and Angela neither answered nor he could hear it resonating in the house, panic brimmed behind his eyes. The idea, the stupid notion of ghosts and phantoms, gnawed at his mind, pushing itself along slowly to the forefront of possibilities. That it was kids playing a prank he had long since given up. The only other suggestion was that some homeless guy or junkie needed somewhere quiet. He dismissed this, too. Both types had places they could easily go, they didn't need to break in anywhere, and besides where would they have got a spare set of keys? So that left...?

Just as he was slowly conceding the fact he might have imagined it, after all, he heard a sound coming from downstairs, faint but audible, and that was all he needed. He rushed down the stairs straining to find the source of what he assumed was Angela's phone.

"Angela, I know you're here. I can hear you. C'mon, stop messing about. I'm not leaving without you."

He checked all the rooms downstairs and when he still hadn't found her, anger seeped into his veins again. He thought about doing the opposite of what he'd said; leave her, fuck her, it was her problem if she wanted to get fired, not his. But another part of him suggested he wait; something wasn't quite right here and it was the cop part of him that insisted he find out what it was. It didn't make sense for Angela to be hiding from him like a criminal. This wasn't a game. He realised something else. Something that made his heart drum a little faster in his chest—the call had ended but he could still hear that same noise, albeit faintly, like a song being played with the volume down very low.

He spun around, considering all the possibilities, then stepped into the hallway. It was slightly louder now, and his eyes drifted towards the small door under the stairs. Whoever he had seen upstairs at the window must be down there. It had to be Angela. It couldn't be a coincidence that he had heard something the second he had dialled Angela. *Could she be hurt*? he wondered. Had she been checking out the house and maybe stumbled upon someone and they had dragged her down there?

His anger at her dissipated rapidly, replaced by urgency and panic. He threw open the door and called down to her. No answer came except the faint jingling of the same tune, accentuating his dread and anxiety. It was pitch black down there, so he fumbled around for a light switch, yet when he found it and no light came on, he cursed and began stumbling down the stairs as best he could. Like most cops, in his jacket pockets he had an assortment of what could be useful tools. One of them was a small torch. He pulled it out and flicked it on, shining it around the basement floor. For a moment, his heart almost leapt out of his mouth when he saw the dried crimson patch on the floor, thinking at first it was Angela's blood, then remembered the girl they found dead down there.

"Angela? You down here? Stop fucking about. Are you hurt?" his voice echoing around the room.

"Shit," he muttered when he received no reply. He crept further down the stairs, his nerves taut like live wires, eyes stinging as he scanned for any movement. Usually he carried a small pocket knife with him as well, yet when he checked it wasn't there. This was the scene that every cop detested—walking into the unknown alone, unsure what to expect and from who. It was times like this he wished the force was issued with guns like their American counterparts.

Doug reached the bottom of the stairs and shone the small beam around, creating ghastly shadows that nearly made him jump every time a new one was created. It was like being surrounded by a dozen shadowy figures, all waiting to attack him. He pointed the torch at the dried pool of blood and was dismayed to see a footprint embedded there. It was small—either a child's or a woman's, with the Nike emblem in the middle. Angela had been here, then. He knew she always wore Nikes on her days off. But where was she now? He could still hear the muffled ring tone, yet now it seemed to be coming from everywhere around him and was impossible to pinpoint its exact location. He headed to the far end of the basement, beam scanning old boxes piled high, looking for the source of the music.

Something dark and fast moved in his peripheral vision. He spun around just in time to see something dart up the stairs. The faint melody suddenly increased in volume until it was screaming in his ears, as though someone had suddenly turned on a set of speakers at full volume. It was a song by Pink Floyd that was howling at him, *Wish You Were Here*. Fear brought on by the deafening music made him rush to the stairs to escape it, and at the same time catch whoever had been hiding down here.

The basement door slammed shut, trapping him.

Blind panic overcame him. He bolted up the stairs and grabbed the door handle, twisting it both ways to no avail. Something stabbed at the back of his head—a finger or something else, something deadlier. He flailed out behind him, gripping the torch harder, not daring to drop it despite the terror that had inflicted his every cell. He screamed as he was pushed hard down the stairs. He landed halfway, the same song repeating over and over again, his eardrums at bursting point. Underneath the door on the opposite side, a shadow moved in the hallway. He scrambled to his feet, rushed back up the stairs again and this time held the torch in his mouth, leaving him in near total darkness but wanting both hands free to tug at the door.

"Open the fucking door!" he screamed. "Let me out!"

Abruptly, the music stopped. Such was the sudden silence, it was almost deafening. Except it wasn't entirely silent. Harsh breathing was blowing into his ear, a foul stench emanating from it like something dead was sitting on his shoulder. He spun around once more. And screamed.

At the bottom of the stairs, he could discern a shadowy figure staring up at him with flames in its tiny eyes. The figure was blurry, no definitive shape to it, but he knew instinctively it was human. It took a solitary step up the stairs towards him, the step creaking despite the formation being translucent and not possessing any tangible weight to it.

Doug was frozen. He knew somehow what he was looking at, yet at the same time his brain tried to convince him it was just absolute terror creating the image before him. It couldn't possibly be because these things didn't exist and Angela was wrong. It was mass hysteria causing this thing to appear and take another step towards him, its eyes fiery and burning, so much that he could feel the heat on his face. But another part of his brain, the part that insisted upon evidence and clues and logical trains of thought, overwhelmed the rest of his emotions and he did the only thing his feral instinct allowed for. He threw his torch at the thing now inches from him, turned and nearly pulled the door handle off in his desperation.

This time the door opened.

He bundled outside, tripping over his feet in his inertia to escape, and ran from the house. He didn't even close the door or look behind him as he jumped in his car and sped off, tires screeching and kicking up dirt and stones.

# Fifteen

Angela didn't think she would be able to sleep. Her whole body was too alert, tingling like she'd had a minor electrical shock, her nerves prickling with static. Her head was even worse. So many images and thoughts crisscrossed each other it was hard to keep track of exactly what she was trying to focus on at each moment. She knew what she *wanted* to think about, but there were too many variables, too many possibilities, too many paths to run down. She had tried to slow down, typing into her laptop each variation of what she believed she had witnessed, where to start, how to end, who to tell, but after just a few minutes all her brain could visualise and focus on was the semi-transparent figure she had seen in the basement, the way it swirled and shimmered, one second almost within touching distance, the next backing off as though she was the ethereal intruder and it couldn't decide how to proceed.

What she had seen earlier surpassed everything she had felt before surrounding her grandmother's death. It wasn't just a playful or curious spirit sadly waving goodbye for the last time. It was the cruel and vengeful spirit of someone who had forced a number of parents to kill their children with absolutely no remorse whatsoever. A phantom serial killer. There was no possibility of feeling any empathy for this spirit. She could not think of a single reason to justify doing what it did. Whoever this had been when alive may have suffered the most terrible of tragedies, but that gave it no right to seek revenge by causing the deaths of innocents.

And then there were the signs it had left that also kept muddling with her thoughts; the police siren, the knife dripping blood that had spelt something like NIKES onto the wall. If the ghost was seeking revenge for something that had happened to it, the brand name of the trainers must play an important part in deciphering the mystery. But this has been going on for over thirty years. Had Nike even started fabricating footwear that long ago? The only thing she could think of was to go through old files and see if there were any suspects bearing anything related to that manufacturer.

She decided that tomorrow at work she was going to confront Doug, tell him everything she knew and use the photo on her phone as confirmation. See what the ignorant fool had to say then. It was while imagining his reaction that she began to smile and was soon asleep. But her dreams were far from restful.

She found herself in the garden of 11 Parkland Drive. Why she was here she didn't know yet felt compelled to be present; something was tugging at her conscience and all she knew was that she couldn't leave. Snakes ran amok in the overgrown grass and weeds, hissing at her as they brushed past. Spiders the size of her hand scurried up the crumbling brickwork. The rose bush in the corner of the garden had thorns longer than her thumbs that were made of steel, so the bush resembled an intricate roll of barbed wire. An owl landed on the awning above the front door, its eyeballs golden flames that sizzled the bird's feathers. It hissed at her then flew off. Snakes coiled at the front door like abandoned hoses, a spider clung to the door handle.

She badly wanted to leave, get out of here, the creatures were telling her in their own way to do so, but she couldn't. Something was in that house, something of vital importance, and she had to go in.

She took a step closer. The spider rose on its eight legs, posing threateningly. She thought it was hissing at her, too. The snakes raised their heads, their tongues flickering in and out, as if tasting her fear. The owl flew back over her head, its sharp talons brushing past her hair, circling her, huge beak snapping in fury. She ignored them all and held out a shaking hand to open the door. The spider refused to budge. She knew that if she touched it while opening the door, it would run up her arm, maybe tangle itself in her hair and bite her, but she had no choice. She wrapped a hand around the door handle, touching the wiry hairs of the spider, its eyes black orbs staring at her, but instead of attacking her, it hissed, and scurried off. The door creaked open.

A gust of foul wind rushed to greet her; a cloud of obnoxious fumes so thick she could taste it. It rushed up her nostrils and down her throat, making her gag as if she'd just inhaled someone's rotting soul. A wailing sound was coming from inside the house, soon joined by another then another, as if Satan had just set up his own demonic team of choir girls. Angela stepped in and surveyed her surroundings. Instead of framed photos of the Tennant family on the walls, they had now been replaced by morbid, black-and-white photographs of all the girls that had died in this house. They sat on chairs or the old sofa, their eyes white marbles, necks twisted at terrible angles. Their parents stood over them smiling, some holding knives, other's lengths of rope. It reminded Angela of the photos of hunters proudly standing beside their latest prey—a lion, an elephant. Blood trickled down the photos from the dead girls' eyes, running down the old, dirty plasterwork and pooling on the floor. Huge flies, the size of mice, skittered in the pools, drowning. The spiders crept from their hiding places and picked them off one by one.

The wailing continued upstairs, haunting in its melody. Trapped souls begging to be released, crying out in sorrow and terror. Beside her, the basement door flew open, crashing against the wall. Then it closed with such force and speed it made the walls and stairs shake. She was about to head up the stairs towards the infernal choir when the basement door opened again and stayed opened. A beam of light came from inside. A warmth emanated towards her, drawing her inexorably towards the door. She hesitated, then followed as though summoned by the invitation.

When she peered down, she saw nothing. No bloodstained floor, no creeping shadows. The basement looked perfectly clean and spacious, the workbench spotless, everything in its designated position, gardening tools hanging from the walls. A young girl's pink bicycle sat at the bottom of the stairs. This was how it had looked when things were normal in here, perhaps when the original owner had bought the place. The light began to fade. Shadows loomed ominously across the floor. Shadows twitched and moved, growing ever larger with each passing moment. Angela gasped when one of the shadows, long and elongated, slowly changed colour; now, instead of black, it turned red, before spilling across the floor like a low tide. It stopped when the perfect outline of a person was created—a child, judging by its size. And then a wail, terrible and piercing, broke the silence. It soon turned to a roar— of some large animal in terror or agony. Objects exploded and shattered, the foundations shook, as another shadow loomed over the bloodied template.

Then came the scream of a girl, oddly familiar. Yet it seemed to be different voices screaming in unison but for different reasons. Among the screams one was begging, "Do it! Do it!" while simultaneously another voice begged her assailant for mercy. Both sounds were coming from above and below and she couldn't tell which was which, although she thought she knew. It was confirmed when the swish of a blade cut through the air and one of the screams abruptly cut off. Fresh blood accumulated on the basement floor. But it was the remaining voice that terrified her.

She turned and ran upstairs but only managed to get halfway before she stopped in horror. As though thrust into the middle of a movie—as an unseen extra—she gasped as she saw a figure dragging Kim by the hair along the hallway. She was kicking and screaming, lashing out, to no avail. The figure dragged her to the top of the stairs with one hand, a long, gleaming knife in the other. His head was drooped downwards and he had his back to her so it was impossible to determine who the assailant was. She tried to run to help, but she was frozen in time, pushing against an invisible boundary.

The figure dragged Kim right past her, as if she wasn't there, loud thuds on the steps, that shook each time Kim bumped down another.

"Kim! It's me. I'm here!" she yelled, yet when she reached for the intruder, her arm went straight through him. She clutched fistfuls of air, kicked at the banister instead of the figure, grabbed a handful of carpet off the stairs instead of her daughter. The two continued past her, completely oblivious to her presence. Tears blurred Angela's vision as desperation and impotence overwhelmed her. She could smell Kim's favourite perfume as she bounced past. That coupled with the sharp stench of urine and sweat. The two reached the bottom of the stairs, Kim still thrashing wildly, howling for her mother, begging him to stop, that he didn't know what he was doing. That he was her uncle.

That was when the figure turned and looked up at Angela. Jimmy's face, a melted wax sculpture, what was left of his brain still throbbing in the hole in his head, shards of bone embedded deep like shrapnel. The side of his head that was missing still bore the socket where his eyeball had once been, a half-moon shape now filled with squirming things that plopped onto Kim's face and body. His remaining eyeball was bulging, ready to pop like an overfilled balloon, dead yet glowing like a dying ember. His jawbone was visible on the left side of his face, blackened teeth gnawing together while on the other side his remaining lips were curled upwards in a parody of a grin. Drool ran in copious amounts from his slippery mouth, dropping onto Kim and sizzling when they hit her soaked pyjamas.

Jimmy tried to say something, but all that came out was a ghastly, sickening wet hiss, a slurping sound that caused more spit to spray the air around them like foam from waves lapping at the shore. It might have been an attempt at laughter; certainly, the gleam in his eyeball suggested he was having a lot of fun. Raucous, gruff sounds came from him—similar to a dog trying to bark with a mouthful of food.

In that instant, her body snapped out of its paralysed state and she was able to run. She saw Kim's body now lying perfectly within the bloodstained shape on the floor, like an outline had been made of her in preparation. The screeching sirens blasted all around her, causing her to almost stumble and fall. For some reason, she held her penknife. It flew from her hand, blood once more pouring from the blade and cascading down onto the concrete like a dirty waterfall. It spun in the air then shot off like a throwing star, embedding itself in the far wall. The sirens suddenly stopped. Replaced by *Wish You Were Here* by Pink Floyd.

Somehow, despite her heightened state, she knew that this was all meant for her, a sign, but she could only focus on rescuing Kim. Who was barely conscious now, lying perfectly still in the bloodied outline of her body, while Jimmy loomed, taunting her with the knife. He squatted beside her and was joined by a dark, shadowy figure who glanced her way, a devilish grin on its translucent face. It was the one who had caused all this, back again to claim another victim. But this wasn't about claiming another; it was about Angela. She was here for a reason, to witness something horrendous, and it was all meant for her unless she did what the ghostly figure demanded. His voice was yelling in her head—*find him. Stop him. Fail to do so and there will be another.*

From nowhere, dark, red patterns appeared on the walls, as if old, rust-coloured water was seeping through the plasterwork. It continued until the word NIKES or something resembling it was formed everywhere. Near blinded with desperation for Kim, she tried to push herself to where the girl lay but her feet were stuck to the concrete. She reached out with both arms while her brother and the dead occupant of the house stared back at her, grinning. Just as Jimmy raised the knife and brought it quickly down onto Kim's frail chest, she woke up.

Panting heavily, she remained this way for a few seconds, then jumped out of bed and dashed to her daughter's room. She burst in, causing Kim to groan and mumble in her sleep, and only stopped when she saw the gentle rise and fall of the blanket. Her heart straining against her flimsy nightdress, it gradually eased its rhythm as she checked to make sure Kim was indeed safe and sound. But her heart rate increased once more when, coming softly from Kim's phone, she heard a tune from the same band—*Run Like Hell*. Angela snatched up the phone and turned it off, before dropping it quickly as though infectious. She barely slept for the rest of the night.

# Sixteen

Once again, Kim opened her eyes and a sense of having been involved in a fight shuddered throughout her body. A fight with a professional boxer or something, because every inch of her body ached. She considered the possibility that she was coming down with the flu but her nose wasn't running, her throat didn't feel as though on fire, and there wasn't a sneeze constantly brewing in her nostrils. It wasn't her period either, so she had no idea why she felt this way. When she moved to check the time, she was shocked to see her phone on the floor and switched off. Kim *never* turned her phone off.

She leaned over, turning it back on and considered what might have happened. Obviously, during the night she had a bad dream, thrashing about maybe, and had inadvertently knocked it off. This might explain why her bones ached. She tried to recall her dream, while still fresh in her memory, but her brain was still half asleep it seemed—fragments of her dream were there, but foggy and unclear, only the slightest of flashbacks which made no sense.

Then they slowly pieced together. She had been in a house,

trespassing. She didn't know how, but she knew it was the house Mum was investigating. It might have been because in her dream she had seen shadows of girls her age wandering around aimlessly, looking sad and dejected. Another figure had appeared and grabbed her, slapping her until she collapsed to the floor. She was suddenly on the stairs, and another person was watching but doing nothing to help despite her screams and lashing out.

She found herself in the basement and more ghostly figures surrounded her like they were going to hurt her. Someone was watching from the stairs like some sick, perverted voyeur, doing nothing to help. The person's face had been half missing, bits of brain and flesh dripping onto the floor like candle wax, yet even so she thought she recognised who it was, despite it being hard to tell from the already fading image. Then a knife was being held over her chest, and…

Kim gasped and sat up—her aching body forgotten about. The person holding the knife had been her mother, grinning insanely, and she was about to make Kim the latest victim. A sudden jolt and noise had brought her from her slumber, waking her momentarily and now, thinking about it, she was pretty sure she remembered opening her eyes to see her mother standing over her for real.

A shudder thundered through her. Now that her head was clearing, she was damn sure her mother had been there, watching her. But why? What had been her motive? Could it be…Was it possible her mother standing there and her nightmare were connected somehow? It was the second nightmare she had involving that house and her mother. She'd read stories when her mother told her she was joining the force about detectives investigating serial killers who had got so involved with cases they had lost a sense of reality, acting out the roles themselves to understand their motives and thinking. Could this case be affecting her mother in the same way?

Strangely enough, rather than scaring her, the more she thought about it, she became more enthralled. Something was going on in her village that had Mum so engrossed, so submersed in, it was making her act weird. After doing a little research on serial killers and discovering a large number had been active in Bradwell and were now in Northgate, she told Chris about it at school one afternoon and a huge grin had surfaced on his face. They had joked about her mother becoming involved in such a case and how they might have inside information if she shared it with them. It looked as if that time might have arrived.

Forgetting all about her aches and pains, she quickly dressed and headed downstairs for breakfast. Her mother was already sat at the breakfast table, holding a mug of steaming coffee, but rather than drink it she was simply staring into the dark water like a clairvoyant reading someone's palm.

"Hi, Mum," she said as she grabbed herself a bowl and cereal and sat down.

Her mother barely acknowledged her. Kim stared at her, thinking she seemed to have aged twenty years overnight. Purple rings circled her eyes, her skin sagged as if incapable of supporting the weight of the burden she evidently carried. Strands of grey hair poked through her scalp like weeds.

"Mum? You okay?"

"Mmm?" she replied looking up suddenly. "Oh! Sorry, I was lost for a minute there. You, umm, sleep well?"

"More or less."

"Good. Don't be late for school. I have to leave early. Make sure you come home straight after as well."

"Come home early? Why? What's wrong?"

"Nothing. I just...don't be late, okay."

Angela finished her coffee and headed upstairs to get ready for work. Kim watched her go, a bubble of excitement creeping up her body as she texted a message to Chris. *U won't believe what I got to tell u. More later.* There, that should get him interested enough.

Her mother finally came down, having added some makeup to hide the purple rings, so at least she was aware she looked like shit. She kissed Kim, told her she loved her, and kissed her again while embracing her and almost sending her bowl of cereal crashing to the floor.

"Hey, you're gonna suffocate me."

Angela managed a smile, kissed Kim's forehead and left.

*Wow*, she thought. *She really is immersed in this case.*

Her phone beeped. *What? Tell me now*, it said.

Kim giggled. She replied with a series of emojis, wanting to tease him. Hopefully he'd be waiting for her at the school gates. She'd be the centre of his attention all day until she told him. When Chris answered with an angry emoji and a series of red hearts, Kim lost her appetite. It was as if a flock of butterflies had woken in her stomach and were softly flapping about. She dumped the rest of her breakfast in the sink, then rushed to get ready. Within thirty minutes she was already at school—a record.

"Hey, Chris," she said when she saw him waiting just as she predicted. Her cheeks were warming already.

"Hi, Kim. So come on, spit it out. What's going on that's got you all excited?"

She thought about telling him then and there; she could barely keep it back any longer, but she promised herself to tease him with it, force him to be around her all day. The other girls would see it and get jealous—Chris with his wavy, blonde hair, and sky-blue eyes. All the girls had a crush on him and she couldn't wait to see their reactions when he would be inevitably hanging around her during lunch break.

"I can't tell you right now, you'll have to wait. But this is gonna seriously freak you out!"

"Aww, c'mon, tell me! What's it about?"

"A case my Mum is working on." And with that Kim refused to tell him any more.

As prophesied, Chris stuck to her like a leech throughout the day, begging for more information. She felt like a goddess being courted by the village prince. Chris tried to prise the details from her by promising all kinds of things, but not what she wanted—to go out together. She wasn't too disappointed—plenty of time for that, yet.

She deliberately avoided telling her best friend, Lisa, until school finished. Lisa went home for lunch anyway, so had no idea what had been going on. When she caught up with her after the final bell and told her she had some amazing information to tell her, she led Lisa to the gates and together they waited for Chris. He was practically running when he saw Kim and she beamed with delight.

"Okay, now you gotta tell me. I'll never speak to you again if you don't."

"What? What's going on?" asked Lisa.

"My Mum. She's been acting really weird lately, like lost, totally out of it, hardly sleeping. Then I heard her talking to her partner the other day. There's this house…"

Kim told them the rest and when she finished her heart was about ready to burst. Chris looked like his eyeballs were about to explode, the grin on his face impossibly wide. Lisa was the same.

"You are fucking kidding me!" said Chris eventually. "How come we never knew about this before? Our own fucking Amityville right here in Bradwell. Shit."

"I know, right? It's weird. It's like it's been covered up or something. I could barely find anything in the newspapers when I searched the history, which considering what happened there should have been on the front page!"

"You know what this means, don't you?" said Chris after a moment's thought.

"What?" said both Kim and Lisa simultaneously.

"We need to check it out, of course! Let's go now."

Kim's smile wavered. "I can't. My Mum said I have to be home early today. This shit is really getting to her, making her all soppy around me. I think she has a key somewhere. We could go at the weekend when she lets me stay out longer."

"Done!" said Chris as he hugged her.

Kim thought she might faint at any second.

# Seventeen

Angela drove absently around the streets of Bradwell paying little attention to what was going on around her. The occasional yell or car horn blaring failed to wake her from her daze; when a car ran through a red light she wasn't in the mood to go chasing after it, either; and when she saw a tussle going on between two men outside a pub she continued driving. One thing and one thing only occupied her mind today.

To her surprise, Doug had phoned in sick, something about having a fever. Since they had teamed up, Doug had never missed a day through sickness and so today she had another companion—one she barely knew and looked to be not much older than eighteen. She couldn't help wondering if there was more to it; if perhaps he was still upset about their argument on Friday. She wouldn't put it past him, he seemed a pretty sensitive guy, hating arguments, blushing even when she poked a little fun at him. She didn't know why he and his girlfriend had split up, although his complete disinterest in kids was probably to blame.

In a way, she was glad. While on one hand she wanted to

show him the photo she'd taken of the word NIKES and tell him about everything else that happened, the clues the spirit had given her, being alone gave her time to think about other, more pressing matters. More serious matters.

Starting with the nightmare she'd had last night. It was the second one involving both Jimmy and Kim in the last week, since going to 11 Parkland Drive, in fact. Ever since Jimmy had died that fateful night, she'd suffered nightmares in which she relived the moment of his death again and again, Jimmy standing there with half his face missing, accusing her of not doing more to save him. She knew it was something she would have to live with; God knows she felt guilty about it already without the grim reminders. Her mother had reminded her of the fact plenty of times as well. It was the main reason she joined the force in the first place; subconsciously, she believed at the time that somehow, in the eyes of God or whoever was watching from above, by trying to make amends for what she had allowed to happen by arresting other criminals, it might help to compensate. And if she could slowly work her way up to the Serious Crimes Unit, capture and arrest more dangerous criminals, see them locked up in Northgate, this would see her path to Heaven laid even clearer before her.

But that was then. Things had changed. She couldn't help but think there was a connection between the nightmares with Kim and the house. The stark realisation she had concluded last night was that unless she found out whatever the spirit was trying to tell her, Kim would be next on its list. There was no other reason she could think of for these nightmares to suddenly start. That ghost, that thing, was warning her. *Solve the clues I have given you or I will be coming for you*. It must be why she had that sudden image of Jimmy the day she and Doug went to the house for the first time to arrest the Tennants. Maybe the spirit had picked up on her memories and was using them against her. Could it be using the ghost of Jimmy to gain access to Kim? Use him as a vessel to traverse time and space? Perhaps it couldn't leave the house and needed help.

It was why she had told Kim to come home straight from school today, but really what did it matter? If her suspicions were correct it wouldn't matter in the slightest. One night, Angela would wake up, her body and mind taken over by this vengeful creature, and she would go to Kim's room, perhaps with a knife in her hand, stand over the girl while she slept, and then...

Doug had tried to warn her. She was getting too involved. It was affecting her mood, her thinking, even her complexion. And hadn't Kim said the same thing the last few days? But she had dismissed both of them as exaggerating. All she had wanted to do was delve a little deeper into why these people were committing such terrible acts. What was forcing them to do it. She knew virtually from the moment she had entered the house the first time that something had been lurking unseen within its walls, that there was no way the Tennants had voluntarily killed their daughter, and now, because of it, she had unwittingly become a potential future victim.

The thought terrified her. It was unconceivable in its magnitude. From the moment Kim had been born, thoughts had returned to Jimmy and how she failed to protect him that fateful day in the supermarket. That she was never going to do the same to her little girl. She would be there for her always, as her mother and best friend. When Terry had left it had broken her heart, not for herself but for her girl who had just lost a father, especially when he failed to keep in contact. Kim was missing not only an uncle, but a father. And now it seemed the unthinkable was on the verge of occurring.

*I'll kill myself first*, she thought as she drove through the outskirts of Yarmouth, ignoring everything that was going on around her.

When a car beeped its horn at her, she glanced in her rear-view mirror to see she had gone through a red light herself and had almost been ploughed into by another car. It was then she realised she was crying and could hardly see where she was going. Angela quickly pulled over and stopped the engine. Her temporary partner asked her if she was okay, and she mumbled something about an ill relative and didn't want to discuss it. He said nothing and looked away, no doubt confused and concerned. She hoped he wouldn't report her behaviour later.

She thought about sending Kim to her mother's, let her stay there for a few days until she solved the mystery. But both of them would want to know why—Angela was just a regular cop, there was no reason to move her daughter out, unless someone was stalking them, and that was another thing altogether. She thought of going to Sergeant Wilmore with her new evidence, get him to reopen the cold cases, but what would he say to that? He'd probably suspend her for breaking and entering and interfering where she didn't belong. Maybe she should go to Doug's house, tell him her fears, show him the photo. Surely he'd decide to help her then? *And what do you think he's going to do? You've already had one argument and he's taken a day off work because of it. He'll probably tell you you should have known better. Keep away from the house and the thing will leave you alone in the process. If it even exists.*

So what did that leave? Other than the most drastic of options? As far as she could tell, she had but one left—resolve the case. She pulled out her phone and scrolled through the photos again, stopping on the bloodied word on the floor. Nikes. It was telling her that whoever the spirit was angry with was related in an important way to this particular brand. It had to be important because pretty much everyone wore Nikes these days. She could hardly go through all the old suspects list and try and find out who owned a pair of Nikes at some point. Maybe it was someone who owned a sport shop. Worked in a factory or was a salesman. Again, the possibilities were endless and fruitless. It would take her weeks.

*The house, Angela. The house. How many people could feasibly know if there were a family living there or not except the neighbours? Maybe Doug is right—you should start closer to home, not out there beyond the stars and other dimensions.*

As if she had been deliberately led out to this part of town, subconsciously or by more ethereal forces, directly opposite her was Hawthorn's Letting Agency in Yarmouth, where they pretty much had a monopoly over rentals in Bradwell and the surrounding areas. And she knew already that the house was leased by them.

*Might as well start now, then.*

She told her partner to stay in the car and climbed out, already mentally preparing a series of questions to ask, and headed inside. She went to the nearest desk and asked to speak to the manager. The girl, looking more than a little concerned, quickly rushed off to tell him. This was a long shot and Angela didn't expect anything to come of it, but figured if she could at least remove him from the list of possibilities, it would be less for Doug to use against her.

But when the elderly-looking man came out of his office and glared at her, her heart thudded with more urgency. If suited businessmen were considered the epitome of heartless folk without a care for their clients, only thinking of making money, this guy must be their ringleader. He was a tall, thin man with short, grey hair, barely a wrinkle on his tanned skin yet with light blue eyes that seemed to burn with intensity. Dressed in an expensive-looking grey suit and dark blue tie he bore the kind of stare that would terrify a person if alone with him on a dark night. His lips looked cold and thin, and she wondered if he had ever smiled in his life. Certainly the lack of age lines around them suggested it might be the case. His initial aura was of someone who had very little pleasures in life other than seeing discomfort in others. *Like a huge, predatory shark*, she thought to herself.

He walked confidently over to her, not bothering to smile. "May I help you?"

The fact she was in police uniform evidently didn't impress or disturb him in the slightest. She noticed the staff giving him nervous glances, then burying their heads in work. Determined not to be intimidated by him, she made herself stand tall and set her gaze firmly on his.

"I was hoping to ask you a few questions about a case I'm working on."

He looked her up and down, as if questioning why a simple uniformed officer might be doing detective work. "I'm busy. Is it important?"

"Yes, it is. I was hoping to have a private chat with you. In your office, maybe?"

He grunted and sighed, clearly unhappy. "As you wish. But you will have to be quick. I have an important meeting soon. Follow me."

She followed him into his office, sneering at him behind his back. *Prick*. He sat behind his large oak desk, not inviting Angela to take a seat, but she sat anyway. Now she was here with him, technically her first suspect, she wasn't quite sure where or how to start. The name on the wooden plaque on his desk said Nikolas Hawthorn. Her blood froze as she thought of the word on the basement wall.

"You wanted to speak with me?" he said, impatiently.

"Yes, umm, I'm looking into a case involving several homicides that occurred over a period of time in the same house. One of your rental properties, 11 Parkland Drive."

Nickolas gave no indication of interest, as if he'd never heard of the place. "What of it?"

"I assume you know there was a homicide last week. The Tennant family. Murdered their daughter."

"Yes, of course. But what does that have to do with me?"

"You've owned and managed this agency for a number of years, I believe?"

"Correct. Almost thirty. Why?"

"So then you are obviously aware of all the other homicides. Did you ever speak to the detectives involved after the first homicide occurred?"

"No, not at all. I was informed of what happened, and the house became vacant a short time afterwards. If the parents admitted to killing their children, why would there be an investigation?"

"And you never thought it bizarre, not to say, morbid, that the same thing has been happening repeatedly over the years? In the same house?"

"Well, yes, of course. I have children myself. Terribly tragic. But all coincidence. Unless you believe the house to be accursed?"

What might have been a scornful look crossed his face. Or an attempt at a smirk.

"And why would you say that? Is that what others believe?"

"I have no idea, officer. My job is to ensure the house is making money, not whether or not it is haunted or...I don't know...built on an old graveyard. Superstitious nonsense." He scoffed.

"What about the serial killer that was stalking the area around the time the first death happened?"

She hoped that by throwing the question in there without warning it might spark some kind of surprised response from him, but all she got was a look of confusion.

"Serial killer? You've lost me."

"Yes. About thirty years ago a number of young females disappeared. Four were murdered, others were never found. The killer was never caught. Do you remember now?"

"Vaguely, I think. That is a long time ago. What does that have to do with anything?"

"You purchased the agency at the same time?"

"It may have been around that time, yes."

"Doesn't it seem kind of coincidental that while a serial killer is murdering children, the same thing started happening in a house you lease? And it always happens to a family with one daughter. Nobody else. Never. Every family that moves in with just a daughter ends up murdering them? Does that make it seem a little more than coincidence, wouldn't you say?"

"Put like that, yes. And I can see where you are going with this. But no one ever came here asking questions related to the murders. Bradwell is a small village, and Yarmouth isn't a very large town, so I'm quite sure everyone was questioned at some point. I do recall the detective that led the task force. Quite a troubled man."

"Do you think the serial killer and the one that killed the girls at Parkland Drive could be the same perpetrator? That the serial killer was not only kidnapping and murdering young teenagers but is also responsible for those that died in the house? The only people, apart from neighbours, who would know when a family with a young daughter moved in would be the agency that rented them the property. Wouldn't you agree?"

There, she'd said it. She was getting desperate now. It was like talking to a brick wall. The man showed no emotion, no interest, as if he couldn't care less.

"Quite a bold statement, officer. You are implying that person might be me or someone who works for me."

"We are considering all possibilities. You owned the agency here at the time. You would know which employees handled the tenancy agreements of that house. You must have records. I'd like to see them."

"Really? Well for that to happen, you would need a search

warrant, of course. I find it curious that you came here as a uniformed officer and not a detective. Why would that be?"

Dammit. He'd called her bluff. To get a glimpse at the records, she would have to explain everything to the Sarge, and she sure as hell wasn't going to do that.

"I can get a search warrant if necessary, but I was hoping you might be more cooperative. Once I have that order our tech department will seize all your computers if deemed necessary. Would you want that?"

"You get that order, then we'll see," he said, offering the beginnings of a smile.

*Bastard,* she thought. *He knows damn well it's not going to happen.* She had no choice but to leave. Maybe one of the guys at the station could do a background search for her.

She stood up, trying to think of something clever to leave him with, but she was too despondent. She had counted on him giving her more. A look of unease, or concern, and had got nothing. As she turned to open the door, she noticed a sports bag, and there next to it on the floor was a pair of Nikes. She quickly looked away, her breath trapped in her lungs. It seemed it was time to finally talk to someone higher up the ladder. Her daughter's life depended on it.

# Eighteen

For the third time, Angela knocked on Kim's bedroom door to ask her if she wanted to watch a movie. Her choice, whatever she wanted. But again, Kim, not even bothering to open the door, called to say no, she was talking to friends on her laptop. It was important, she said.

Angela's heart felt like someone had gripped it with an icy hand and was squeezing it tightly. It pained her terribly that all she wanted to do was spend time with her, but Kim was slowly drifting away. She was either out with friends or hidden in that damn room, and she only came down for dinner because Angela refused to let her eat in there as well. As the evening wore on, she was terrified of going to bed, having another of those insidious nightmares, not trusting herself to wake up in time. What if tonight was the night when the thing from that house came into her mind and made her do something terrible? She couldn't even begin to understand how the malevolent spirit would manage to traverse halfway across the village and get into her head, but she couldn't take the risk. She'd stay up all night if she had to, or handcuff herself to the bed. Now, when she needed to be with Kim more than ever, not realising the immense danger she might be in, she was further than she'd ever been. She had to speak to someone tomorrow about the agency. Present all the evidence they had so he was brought in for questioning. Although, she had to confess, Nickolas Hawthorn didn't appear the type to fold easily under pressure. After thirty years, the chances of there being anything to arrest him with were slim.

Angela thought of pouring a glass of wine for her nerves but was worried about falling asleep early, so decided to grab her laptop and try and do a little digging herself. She was about to open it when there was a knock on the door. Surprised at someone knocking so late, she peered out the curtain first and was even more surprised to see Doug standing there. She wasn't sure if she was glad or not—maybe he'd come to try and talk her out of continuing her investigation. *Too late now,* she told herself, and tense at the possibility of a confrontation, went to open the door.

"Hi, Doug. Listen, I..." She stopped. She had been about to apologise for the other day and ask how he was, when she caught the look in his eyes. The pallor of his skin in the light above the porch. He looked like he'd hardly slept.

"Doug, are you okay? Now it's your turn to look like shit."

He forced a weak smile. "Can I come in?"

"Sure. But not if you are contagious, I don't want me or Kim coming down with any—"

"No, I'm not. Not like what you mean, anyway."

Curious, she stepped aside and let him in. "Can I get you anything? Coffee, water, something stronger?"

"Something stronger. Thanks."

Angela led him to the living room, for once glad Kim was in her room, and poured him a large brandy.

"Here, take this."

"Thanks."

He took the glass and gulped down half the contents. She

had never seen him like this and was worried. Had his day off work been more than some bug? Something more serious?

"What is it, Doug? What's wrong?"

He stared at her for a few seconds as she sat beside him, shaking his head as if unsure what to say or whether he should even say it. He opened his mouth to say something but instead took another gulp of brandy and set the glass down.

"Sorry," he said finally.

"Sorry for what?"

"Sorry for...well, dunno, I mean, you have to see things from my point of view. You couldn't possibly expect me to believe what you were saying. I mean, I thought what with those horrible murders, and you being a mother..."

"What is it, Doug? Just say it."

He took a deep breath. "Yesterday, I planned on coming here to speak to you. Get you to see reason. Not just for your health but for your job, too. If the Sarge finds out...So I got in my car, was gonna turn up without warning. I thought that after our argument on Friday you wouldn't want to see me, anyway, so I just headed this way. But for some reason, I decided to go past that house again. Just drive down the road, turn around at the bottom and leave. Why, I don't know. Well, maybe now I do. Maybe it was all that extrasensory stuff you go on about."

Angela could feel her skin tighten as her nerves stretched. Her intestines writhed like worms in her stomach. She thought she had an idea where this was going already.

"So I drove past the house, turned around and...I saw someone peering out from behind a curtain in the upstairs bedroom."

A chill stung Angela's spine.

"I thought it was you, and I was really pissed because I just knew you'd been going in there alone. I noticed you take the spare set of keys to that house. So I went in, determined to drag you out and threaten you with telling the Sarge, but..."

"You saw something, didn't you? Heard things? You go down to the basement?"

He nodded, gulped several times.

"I know, Doug. I've seen it too. What I saw was my dead brother, Jimmy, in there, and...other things."

She grabbed her phone and searched for the photo of the word NIKES. "Look. I took this in the basement. I went there on Saturday, not Sunday."

She told him about the sirens, her penknife flying across the room, dripping with blood and spelling the word on the wall, the song lyrics.

"So tell me what you saw and heard."

Doug was paler than ever now, to the point Angela wondered if he might lean over and puke on her carpet. His hands were shaking terribly. He told her what had happened to him, having to stop several times while Angela filled his glass again and he took several sips. When he finished, he looked at her with what might have been embarrassment on his face, as though he'd just told her something that warranted a lengthy spell in Northgate Hospital for the Mentally Impaired. She guessed, knowing him as she did, that this was what he was probably thinking.

She told him about going to the agency. How there was a pair of Nikes by Hawthorn's desk, how his name was remarkably similar to the word NIKES. Doug's eyes widened.

"You think it is him, then? It was just a half-hearted suggestion to get you to stop thinking about the other stuff. How stupid of me. I thought you were losing it. I think I might be losing it. I mean, vengeful ghosts making people kill children. What the fuck?"

"I know it sounds hard to believe, Doug, but we both heard and saw the same thing. It's trying to tell us something, give us clues. And..." She hesitated, a sob caught in her throat as she thought about Kim and the danger she might be in. She told him about her nightmares and what she thought might happen if they didn't solve the case.

Doug's face took on a greenish hue. His eyes were practically bulging, his bottom jaw resting on his chest. In other circumstances, he might have looked comical.

"Fuck," he whispered, licking his lips, then finishing the remainder of his brandy. "Jesus. So what do we do? I mean, the Sarge is not gonna believe a word of what we say without evidence. And not just the picture on your phone. So let me get this straight; you think the owner of the agency might be the serial killer and somehow also be the one killing those kids in that house?"

"No, Doug. I think he might be the serial killer, but it is the spirit in that house that forces the parents to kill their kids. Maybe something happened to the spirit when it was alive. Maybe it's a victim of the serial killer and they returned to seek revenge. The similarities are too damn close."

If it was at all possible, Doug's eyes bulged even further. "Shit, I forgot to tell you. I phoned in sick because I couldn't focus, so I spent the day doing a little research. Should have done it before, of course, but we didn't know then what we know now. I found out who owned the house during the time the serial killer was stalking Bradwell. You won't believe what I found."

Now it was Angela's turn to stare wide-eyed at him. But before he could tell her, she grabbed his glass, hurried to fill it for him and poured one for herself. She needed it. Both took long sips.

"One of the serial killer's victims was Suzy Glazer. She was found assaulted and strangled near Fritton Woods. Her father, Joe, was a prominent builder—owned the largest construction firm in Yarmouth. His wife died from cancer the year before, so when Suzy was murdered he was grief-stricken. He committed suicide shortly after when they failed to catch the killer. A year later was the first homicide, Mr Hannington's daughter, who we visited in Norwich."

"Oh my God," muttered Angela. "It's him! That's the spirit haunting the house. That explains everything. He must have been so consumed by grief and rage that when he died his spirit lived on and decided to inflict revenge on every other parent that lived in his house until the killer was caught. All we need to do is catch the original killer. We need to go to the Sarge. Before…before something happens to Kim."

A sob lodged in her throat. She couldn't believe it. Her head was spinning. They could finally put a name to the thing haunting the house. Yet the more she thought about it, the harder it became to understand how Joe could do such a thing. Yes, he must have been stricken with grief and anger but why make innocents suffer as he had? As she herself might do? He knew the pain those parents would go through—what kind of a man could do that to someone else?

"What do we tell him?" he asked. "That Joe Glazer's spirit is forcing parents to kill their kids and won't stop until his own daughter's killer is caught? Oh, and by the way, we believe the killer could be the owner of the letting agency that rents out the house. What, you know him? On personal terms with him? Been a friend for years? Of course, we'll go clear out our lockers.

"That's what's going to happen, Angela. And you know it."

She muttered a curse under her breath. As much as she didn't want to admit it, Doug was right. In a small town like this, business owners and high-ranking officers were probably good friends, getting together at Christmas for a drink, helping each other out with 'favours'. Without proof, something other than the photo on her phone, they would get nowhere.

She thought about her nightmares, seeing Jimmy in them,

the weird feeling she'd had the first time she stepped into the house. Maybe it wasn't the Sarge they needed, after all.

"Okay, then, you're right. But I still think Kim could be in danger if we don't do something."

"And what's your idea?"

"You religious, Doug?"

"Me? Hell no. Last time I went to a church was my christening. Why?"

"What do you know about exorcisms?"

# Nineteen

Their shift the next day was a stressful one. They were called to a house where a woman had phoned to say she'd been assaulted by her husband. When they arrived, the woman had several nasty looking bruises on her arms and face, including a swollen eye that was already turning an ugly purple. Apparently, it hadn't been the first time, but now the woman feared for her life—her husband was drunk and this time had gone too far. Just as they were trying to comfort the hysterical woman and get ready to take her to hospital, the husband returned. Furious that she had phoned the police, he attacked them as well. It had taken all their strength to subdue him, receiving a few punches in the process, plus more than a few whacks across the head from Doug's truncheon. At one point, Angela thought Doug was going to fracture the man's skull. She had been both shocked and pleasantly surprised by his ferocity. She didn't think he had it in him.

"Yeah, well, things have been a bit tense lately. I guess he paid for it. He deserved it, anyway, the arsehole."

Angela started seeing Doug in a new light. He wasn't completely impassive about everything, as she had come to believe. The man had feelings and emotions locked up in that pretty little head of his. It just took something extraordinary to unlock them. The thought made her blush and quickly turn her head so he couldn't see.

When their shift ended, Doug suggested they go for a drink, but Angela wanted to get back to researching. She suggested a compromise—grab a few beers and head back to her place. Besides, she didn't like the idea of Kim being on her own. Which was ironic, she had to admit, because what terrified her more was not Kim accidently burning the house down or something stupid, but what she might do. Was Joe watching her now, preparing to force her into doing something horrific? As she arrived home with Doug beside her, a shudder rippled through her as she considered the possibilities. Ever since deciphering the origin of the deaths at Parkland Drive, she had been gripped by fear. A solid, tangible feeling that wrapped itself around her spine and clung to her like a wet shroud. Would it happen tonight? Tomorrow? Was Joe's spirit preparing itself right now to put insidious thoughts into her head? She knew they were close to solving the case, tantalisingly so, but it was like searching for invisible blood stains at a murder scene, but this time instead of using Luminol, it was either a bible, crucifix and holy water or their ingenuity at connecting the crime scenes. When Angela suggested visiting the local priest about a possible exorcism, Doug scoffed and suggested that if Sergeant Wilmore found out, she'd find herself in Northgate before the day was over.

But it wasn't his daughter at risk, of course. He wasn't the one terrified of going to bed at night in case something happened. It was also why she had tentatively asked him if he wouldn't mind staying the night, in the spare bedroom. Something told her it was important he did. Fortunately, he agreed. He had managed to grab the original Serial Killer Task Force files. With Kim at a friend's house, they settled down, files spread all over her coffee table, and they browsed through them.

"There's one thing I never fully understood about the task force and the arrests made at Parkland Drive each time a new victim was reported," said Angela after a while. "The task force was made up of ten people and the head detective was Chris Miles. All of these reports I'm looking through are signed by him. Yet these other files show he was also the detective called out to the early homicides on Parkland Drive. Don't you think that's funny?"

"Funny, why?" asked Doug, as he finished his beer.

"Well, don't you think he had enough to do tracking down a serial killer without investigating these cases as well? The task force must have been taking up all his time, so why bother with these seemingly open and shut cases that had been confessed to? Anyone could have gone, like we did."

"Well, I imagine he must have considered a possible connection. Young girls being murdered in two separate locations—the coincidences would be obvious. Just as you figured. We've already been over this."

She continued reading the reports. "But there's nothing that indicates any suspicions connecting the cases. According to this he never even questioned the parents about the serial killer murders. This Hannington case—the first after Joe Glazer committed suicide— says he found the body in the basement, the parents confessed, they were arrested, case closed. Nothing about interrogating them regarding the serial killer. That would have been the first thing I or any other detective would have done, surely?"

"Like I said, Angela. The parents confessed. Why would he think there's a connection? The MOs were different. The relationship to the victims was different."

"I know, but..."

She thought for a moment. There was something wrong

about the details. They had gone to interview the girl's father. He'd gone into detail about what happed to their daughter, until eventually he'd suffocated her with a pillow in her bed. It hit her.

"Look. It says he found the body in the basement. Hannington said he smothered her with a pillow while she was laid in bed. Detective Miles is lying."

Doug glanced over at the report and quickly skimmed it. "You're right. But maybe the father was lying and didn't want to admit he'd dragged her down to the basement."

She ignored him and turned to the other case files. All were vague, the details sparse. Just enough to satisfy Miles' boss at that time. It was clear, as Doug suggested, that the detective hadn't been that interested in these multiple homicides and had written the bare necessities. Finding no other inconsistencies, she picked up a file on the serial killer hunt, hoping and praying there would be something useful in there. Her heart sank as she scrolled through a list of possible suspects at the time, which was depressingly sparse. A few locals who already had criminal records. One guy who had been in prison for attempted murder but was still in prison when the girls had been killed. The absence of the agency owner's name left her deflated. Then, her heart leapt to her throat. There was a photo. One of the few clues the task force had. It was a shoeprint beside the body, showing the unmistakable Nike logo on the sole.

"My God, look."

She handed it to him. Doug stared at it for a while, eyebrows furrowed, then looked at Angela. "Do you have any idea how many people where Nikes? I own a pair myself, so do you. *Everyone* wears Nike stuff."

"Yeah, like the agency owner."

A thought occurred to her. She checked the time. It was still only a little after five. Kim wouldn't be home until nine.

"Let's go see him."

"Who? The agency owner? He'll have us arrested for harassment. We'll—"

"No. The detective. Miles. It's still early, Kim won't be back for a while, we've got plenty of time."

Doug held his head in his hands, then sighed. "And what exactly are you going to say to him? The man's retired—he probably can't even remember half the details anymore."

"An unsolved serial killer case he was in charge of? Kids being murdered at the same time in the same village at the same house? If this man is any kind of cop, it should be haunting his dreams. I just want to ask if he investigated the agency owner or had any reason to suspect him. What he thought might have really been going on at the house. It won't take long—I have to be back for Kim. Remember, this isn't just about finding the serial killer. If I'm right about what I suspect, it's to save my daughter, too. We either try and figure this out or we get an exorcist in, or…"

She never finished the sentence. She didn't have to.

"Okay, okay. Let's do it."

Retired Detective Chris Miles lived just outside the town, twenty minutes away. They hadn't bothered to phone and warn him of their arrival. Angela had the strange idea he would not appreciate the visit, to relive old memories, perhaps even feel certain shame at not solving the case. Seeing as they were out of uniform, they decided to pass themselves off as detectives. Chris Miles would be in his late seventies by now—hopefully he wouldn't think to ask too many questions himself.

Fortunately, there was a light on when they pulled up outside his house. Doug gave her his best '*I really don't want to be doing this*' glare, which she returned with a smile, and together they walked down the garden path. Angela tapped on the door and both took out their badges. After a while, when she was about to knock again, the door opened. Angela had to force a smile on her face.

The man behind the door wore no smile himself, only a scowl, as if he had been rudely interrupted. He was a short, skinny man, with a bald scalp and a few wild strands behind his ears. Liver spots and scabs dotted his shiny bald patch like mole hills in a field. His pale skin was covered in wrinkles, suggesting a life that had presented a lot of stress and hardship, but his eyes were what almost made Angela take a step backwards. They were a piercing, icy blue colour that showed no signs of emotion except perhaps distrust and resentment. A wart sat on the end of his nose like a resting fly. Angela had the idea the serial killer case might have got to him more than she thought.

"What do you want?" he almost growled. "If you're here to sell me anything, you can get the hell off my property now."

He was wearing dirty, brown pyjamas and torn slippers, and held a cigarette in his hand, ash dropping to the floor, his fingers a dirty, nicotine-stained yellow. Angela immediately disliked the man.

"Mr Miles?" said Doug, seeing as Angela failed to say anything. "I'm Detective Doug Ramsey and this is my partner, Detective Angela Harford. We hope we're not disturbing you, but we wanted to ask you a few questions about a case you were working on a few years ago."

Miles' scowl thickened as he glared suspiciously at them and their badges. Angela was already having doubts. This man wasn't going to help anyone. She had the idea that during his career he had probably made a lot of enemies, both within and outside the force.

"What case?" he practically spat. "Can't you see I'm retired? I have been for years."

"The unsolved serial killer case from the early nineties. You led the task force," said Angela, then silently cursed herself for not being more tactful.

Miles' eyes squinted, as if considering the case or trying to remember it. The look of distrust on his face was even more evident.

"What about it? That was a long time ago. You found him, have you?"

It was getting cold now, as the sun gradually set behind them. She really didn't want to have to stand on this man's doorstep to discuss the case, but he showed no intention of letting them in.

"No, we haven't, but a series of recent events have meant we're looking into it again. Could we come in and ask you a few questions? It's quite important."

Chris Miles obviously did not want to let them in. She could almost hear the cogs in his head trying to figure out a reason not to do so. When she was sure he was going to say no, he grumbled and stepped aside, opening the door wider.

"Make it quick," he said.

They both thanked him and stepped in. As he led them to his living room, the smell of tobacco was strong, dust clung to everything and there was an old musty odour, as if he hadn't opened the windows in years to let fresh air in. She didn't know what kind of pension he was on but it was obviously not a very good one—his furniture looked almost as old as him. No sign of any family, either—no framed photos of loved ones, no ring on his finger, nothing to suggest he had ever been married or had kids, which contradicted what they'd been told earlier. A fat, old-looking cat lay sprawled out on an old armchair, purring softly. *At least he has appreciation for some living things,* she thought.

Doug and Angela sat on two chairs by an old dining table while Chris groaned as he slowly eased himself onto the sofa. She wondered if he had arthritis.

"So, what is it then? What happened? That case has bugged me for years. Only one I never solved. They say he died or moved away, but that don't make it any easier. You found new evidence?"

Doug glanced at Angela. *Go on. You brought me out here. You ask him.*

She coughed nervously. "Well, we were looking through the old case files. We noticed there were very few suspects, and those that were on the list were soon discarded. We were wondering if there was anyone else, perhaps someone you always suspected but could never find anything on?"

Miles scratched his bald head, then stubbed out his cigarette. A bout of coughing ensued, momentarily worrying Angela that he was going to have a fit.

"Damn, fuckin' things," he spat. He shook his head. "Nope. Everyone we suspected had alibis. Weren't no evidence anyway, just a shoeprint by one of the victims. We questioned almost everyone in the village but came up with nothin'."

How was she going to lead this towards the agency owner? There was only one way. "At the time of the serial killings there was another series of child murders in the village. All in the same house, 11 Parkland Drive. You investigated those as well. Can you tell us why?"

He stared at her for a while, as though scrutinising her. She felt like he was reading her mind and thoughts. It was the closest she'd ever come to feeling violated. Instinctively, she zipped up her jacket further.

"Well, we figured there might be a connection, somehow. Seemed bloody coincidental to have two sets of child killers at the same time. But all the parents admitted to killing the kids, so we thought no more of it. Should have brought back the death penalty for 'em. Killing kids—it ain't right."

It was so mechanical the way he said it—not a hint of emotion in his voice.

"There was another death last week. A young girl just like

the others. Didn't it make you wonder why so many girls were killed in that same house over the years?"

"Yeah, course it did, but as I said, the parents all admitted to it. They were charged and sent to prison. I didn't like that house. Had a weird vibe, so I kept away."

"The only person who would know that a family had moved into that house with a daughter—except neighbours and friends—would be the owner of the letting agency, a Nickolas Hawthorn. He's still the owner. Did you ever consider him?"

"Like I said, back then Bradwell was a smaller village than it is now, so yeah, everyone was questioned about the serial killings. I rented a house from Hawthorn back then, just after he'd started the agency. Didn't like the guy. Thought he was better'n everyone else. All posh and formal. Refused to give me discounted rent on the place, too, when I knew damn well he did for others on the force."

Miles sat back and thought for a moment, a shrewd look in his eyes, as if considering some secret thought. Then he sat up and looked straight into Angela's eyes. "Yeah, I always had my suspicions about him. He said he had alibis, which we checked out, but they were feeble like he was with a friend one night, and with his wife another. Of course; they were goin' to vouch for him. The friend who verified his whereabouts was his secretary. Said they had a late business meeting, but I thought they were having an affair. Didn't add up what she said. And Hawthorn showed not the slightest bit of upset about the kids being killed. And he had a pair of Nikes that matched the print next to the body. Said he went to the gym on a regular basis. But when we spoke to them, they said he only came once or twice a week; he told us he went at least four times. So yeah, he was on the suspect's list. Why, you found anything out about him?"

"Just a hunch," said Angela and smiled.

Miles grunted. "Yeah, well, I said enough anyway. Don't

you go telling him I said anything about him. If you find who did it, you let me know."

He pushed himself to his feet, indicating the interview was over. Doug and Angela rose, too, and thanked him for his time.

"Don't suppose you found any new evidence, have you?" he asked just as they stepped outside.

"No. Nothing yet, but we're working on it," said Angela.

Miles grunted and closed the door. As Angela started the car, she caught a glimpse of him watching them from behind the curtains.

# Twenty

Angela, Doug, and Kim shared a Chinese takeaway that night, while Doug kept Kim entertained with stories about his short career as an officer so far. All three cracked up when he told her about seeing Angela rugby tackle a guy to the ground after trying to run off with stolen goods; how one day she'd singlehandedly climbed a large tree to rescue an old lady's cat, splitting her trousers in the process and revealing her backside; sprinting after a dirty old man for daring to pinch her butt as he rode past on his pushbike. The laughter abruptly stopped when Kim asked about the house on Parkland Drive.

"Why do you ask?" asked a surprised Angela.

"I just heard some kids talking about it at school. They said it was haunted and loads of people had died there."

"What, and you believe them? The only haunted house around here is this one. I think that's why I keep finding dirty laundry lying everywhere except where it's supposed to be. Why the biscuit tin is always empty when I go to grab one. Yeah, this house is haunted alright. You tell your friends about that."

Kim blushed. "You're the one who eats all the biscuits! They're bad for my complexion. But someone died there last week, didn't they? I heard loads of people have died there. The house makes people kill their kids."

"Kim, that's bull. And morbid. Don't believe everything you hear. It's just a house."

"My friend, Chris, said he saw people looking at it this morning. You think they'll die if they move in?"

Angela was stunned. She'd forgotten about that. There was no way it would be vacant for very long. What then? Hawthorn didn't give a shit about the house's reputation—Miles had said so himself—so at the first opportunity he would have potential tenants viewing the place. They needed to solve this case and fast. And she hadn't been joking when she suggested an exorcism.

"Don't be morbid, Kim. And what was this Chris doing there anyway?"

"He, err, has a friend that lives on that road. They meet before going to school. He told me earlier."

Angela was still stunned at what Kim had said about the prospect of another family looking at the house. Tomorrow she was going to have to go past and check the lock.

The rest of the evening was more subdued. Angela could see in Doug's eyes he was concerned as well, but they said nothing until Kim had gone up to bed.

"Are you thinking what I am?" she said as soon as Kim had left.

"Yes. That arsehole letting agent isn't going to wait around. I bet he's already trying to start proceedings so he can rent it out again. Regardless of whether the renters have kids or not. Miles said he suspected him, but there's nothing connecting him to any of the cases except a circumstantial shoeprint. If he was lying about going to the gym, it was probably because he was seeing his lover and didn't want the wife to find out. Miles should have taken him in for questioning, regardless. Doesn't matter who he is—his alibi was false, that's reason enough."

"We need to get back in that house, Doug."

"Why would you want to go back? The place is dangerous. This Joe, or at least his spirit, has given us clues. The word on your phone must mean Nickolas. Perhaps it was supposed to say Nikes with an apostrophe. As in Nike's is the killer. Nike's —Nick. We just gotta prove it. I say tomorrow we go to Sergeant Wilmore and tell him what we know. Let the Serious Crime Unit take over."

No way. With Kim being potentially involved, Angela was not going to forget about it, regardless of whether the SCU took over or not. Her daughter's life could be on the line, and nothing else mattered.

"No. I can't do that. This is too personal for other reasons," she said. "Anyway, I'm off to bed. You know where the spare room is. There's beer in the fridge, brandy in the cabinet. Make yourself at home."

Once more, she knew that she was going to have a hard time getting to sleep. Her head felt like a meteor hurtling through space, sizzling her brain cells with each nefarious, terrible notion that whizzed past so fast she couldn't focus on any single one. What if someone else died in that house and they hadn't done anything to prevent it? What if they found nothing to connect Hawthorn to the murders? What if Joe Glazer made her do something against her will? What if Miles was lying? She sensed an underlying current of resentment in that man. Against everything and everyone. As if the world had acted against him in some cruel, horrible way and he hated them all for it. What on Earth had made him want to become a detective she had no idea. Probably the feeling of authority and power bestowed upon him. Maybe he'd been bullied as a kid and wanted a little payback, because the overall feeling she had was that he had not been a nice man in his younger days. It showed in his eyes.

And yet, possibly due to simple mental exhaustion, she soon found herself drifting off to sleep.

She found herself in a familiar place. Somewhere she had visited on a regular basis, both in her sleep and in her waking thoughts. She was in the supermarket with Jimmy, boisterous as always, trying to fill the trolley with at least two of all his favourite things. They were joking and laughing, although she was getting a little tired of having to keep removing everything he dumped there. She was only eighteen, she shouldn't have to take care of her brother. While her friends were out partying she was burdened with taking care of things she never expected to.

Her phone buzzed in her pocket. She pulled it out and saw a message from Doug, but the photo of him was around her age, still a teenager. When she answered, a hoarse croaking sound came, like someone with severe asthma struggling to get their words out. She asked him what was wrong, but as she listened the sound grew louder and faster, until it was deafening, and she threw the phone to the floor. But still it intensified until it echoed around the whole supermarket, drowning out all other sounds. She turned to look for Jimmy and get the hell out of there, but he had gone. She called his name, but she might as well have whispered it because nothing could be heard over the manic, animalistic wheezing. Everyone else in the shop seemed completely oblivious to it, carrying on with their shopping as if nothing was wrong. Chatting and laughing with each other.

Panic wrapped her in icy arms. She stumbled blindly down the aisles, her hands covering her ears, screaming for Jimmy even though she knew she could not be heard. Then the noise from her phone stopped. Replaced by a song. Every Breath You Take by The Police, but it kept repeating *I'll be watching you* over and over, and another noise came from further ahead.

From her phone, still lying on the floor, jerking and vibrating as if it was coming to life, came her daughter's voice. It was distant, hard to hear, as if Kim was standing outside and yelling from behind thick panes of glass, but she sounded troubled, the tone in her voice urgent.

Instantly forgetting about Jimmy, she picked it up. "Kim? Is that you? What's wrong?"

But the distant wailing wasn't coming from the phone—it was coming from somewhere else in the supermarket. She dropped her phone again and called out. An elderly woman absently browsing looked up at her and smiled. Her lips cracked as she did so and blood trickled down her chin.

"Have you seen Kim?" she yelled at her. "My daughter. She's lost. I need to find her."

But the old lady ignored her. Her mouth opened wider and blood pooled from it like a waterfall, covering the woman's chest. Angela ran.

As she continued searching for Kim, she heard a commotion at the entrance. Thinking it was Kim calling her, she turned around and ran back, then abruptly stopped. Two men wearing balaclavas stood near the front. They were carrying machetes and threatening the cashier. Angela watched as the cashier gave them the money from the till, but it seemed this wasn't enough. One of the armed robbers slit her throat, laughing as blood splattered the walls and floor and the woman slumped to the floor.

Her police instincts kicking in, she decided to confront them, or at least try to get close enough that she might determine some identifiable features about them.

Kim suddenly walked past them, holding hands with Jimmy. His face seemed to be melting, thick reddish sludge running down one side like a mudslide and hitting the floor with a resounding plop.

"Kim? Jimmy?" she whimpered.

Both stopped and faced her. Kim's expression was of utter dejection, tears streaming down her face, while Jimmy's was of rage, his remaining eyeball bulging, what was left of his lips curled up into a menacing sneer. He pointed at her, then the side of his destroyed face. *You did this. This was you.*

Angela went to go to them, not understanding why Kim was a part of this, when one of the robbers grabbed her around the throat and dragged her backwards, his machete against her throat.

"Let her go!" she howled. "Give me back my daughter. I need to protect her from the house."

But the two armed men laughed at her, as did Jimmy, no attempt on his behalf to help. Kim, who now instead of looking terrified and sad as before, was grinning insanely.

The man holding her slowly drew his machete across her throat.

Angela screamed.

A scream was still bubbling on her lips as she sat bolt upright in bed.

It took her several seconds to realise where she was, but her terror was not put at ease through understanding it had just been another nightmare. Because this wasn't a simple nightmare, she knew that already, but a warning. The beginning of something that would quickly spiral out of control if she didn't figure this out soon. How long before it was her with the knife in her hand?

Now feeling more scared than ever, she decided to check on Kim. Hoping and praying the girl was fast asleep, she opened the door and peered in. Her heart rate slowed down— she was snoring gently, mumbling to herself in her sleep. Angela let out a relieved breath and was about to go back to bed when Kim's arm popped out from underneath the blanket. There was something dark on her arm, long and thin, that wasn't the rolled up sleeve of her pyjama top. Curious, Angela tiptoed over to the bed and touched the dark material. It was wet. When she held her hand up and checked her fingertips, she nearly passed out in her shock. The long, thin strip on her arm was a gash, on Angela's fingers fresh blood.

# Twenty-One

When Angela opened her eyes, her first thought was that she must have fainted. She was slumped in Kim's chair, and when she sat up her neck and spine creaked like a rusty hinge. Outside the sun was slowly making its way over the horizon, clearing the sky of the dark, cloudy blanket hovering above. It took her a few seconds to remember why she was here. Her brain waking from its slumber she stood up, swayed momentarily from the sudden movement, and went to her still sleeping daughter. She gently pulled back the blanket and winced when she saw Kim's arm. It didn't look like a deep cut or Kim would surely have woken and screamed, but the blood was now matted to the blanket, making it look far worse than it was. It seemed more of a nasty scratch than anything else, and Kim did pride herself on having long fingernails, but it seemed highly unlikely such a long scratch could come from that.

Maybe she was just trying to kid herself that it was self-inflicted. She could still vividly recall the nightmare she had, the long blade of the machete slicing across Kim's neck.

What the hell could she do to prove Hawthorn was the

serial killer? There had to be something. A clue they'd missed. Miles had come across as someone who might not have given everything he had to find the killer. When speaking to him he

seemed almost as apathetic to the victims and their families, like the only thing that really mattered had been his pride. But he also said he had issues with Hawthorn, that he hadn't been given the same privileges as others when it came to his rental agreement, so if he had the slightest inkling Hawthorn was involved, surely, he would have given his all to convict him?

There was a knot in Angela's stomach, wrapped around her intestines, twisting ever tighter with each passing moment. She had forced herself to eat the Chinese takeaway last night, to keep up appearances, because really, she felt that every time she ate something she would puke it back up, such were her nerves.

The clock on Kim's wall said it was nearly seven. She would begin stirring soon and if she woke to see her sitting there, she would be worried, wanting to know what was going on. Besides, day shift started soon, and right now she needed coffee. Hopefully Doug would be awake and have fresh coffee brewing. She pulled her daughter's blanket back up and headed downstairs.

"Morning!" said Doug, as she stepped into the kitchen. The strong aroma of caffeine wafted up her nostrils, a firm replacement for any idea of having breakfast—her stomach couldn't take it. She poured herself a large, black coffee and sat down at the table.

"Jesus, do you ever actually sleep at night? You don't look so good."

She told him about her nightmare and the cut on Kim's arm.

He was silent for a while, considering what she'd said. Then he took a sip of his coffee and said, "You don't really think there's a connection here, do you? Like you said, she probably cut herself with a fingernail. I mean, those things on her hands are like talons. I'm surprised she hasn't done herself more damage."

"I don't know if it was or not, but what I do know is that time is running out. Unless we figure a way to put Hawthorn at the scene of one of the crimes, it's not going to stop, Doug. And you know what I mean when I say that. I was thinking about Miles. I picked up a funny vibe from him, like he wasn't genuinely upset about not solving the case. Makes me think that maybe he didn't put as much effort into solving the murders as he could have. He looked mean, cold hearted. No photos of his wife or kids. I get the sense they left him a long time ago."

"Christ, you picked up all that just from listening to him for ten minutes?"

"I told you I pick up on things sometimes. People's auras, whether they're lying or not. That kind of thing."

"So you think he was lying, or just wasn't as committed as he made himself out to be?"

"C'mon, Doug. A tiny village like this and they couldn't catch the guy? It was going on for a while so it definitely wasn't someone passing through that killed those girls. Someone, somewhere, had to have seen something."

"Well, if you're right, they did. Our friendly spirit, Joe Glazer. Can't you make contact with him somehow, get him to write the killer's name down or something?"

"I thought about that, and I tried when I last went. Joe tried to tell me who did it. He left those clues remember, but we don't have anything putting Hawthorn at the scene or any evidence linking him."

"Then I don't think we have much choice but to go to Sarge Wilmore and tell him what we suspect."

"Ugh. And he'll probably put us on traffic duty for the next two months."

Just then they heard noise coming from upstairs. A door slammed and Kim came running down the stairs.

"Mum! Mum, what the hell, Mum?"

She burst into the kitchen, her bloodied arm held in the air and away from her body as though it contained something highly poisonous and contagious.

"I know. I poked my head in your room last night and saw it. You must have scratched yourself. Does it hurt?"

Angela tried not to show how worried she was, and there was no way she was going to tell Kim what she thought was the real reason behind the wound on her arm, but it was difficult.

"No, it doesn't hurt that much, but my bed is covered in blood! And it wasn't a fingernail either. It's gross!"

"Then what else was it? Maybe it's time you cut them back a little. Look at them."

"No! It took me ages to grow them this long."

Angela glanced at Doug who said nothing, lost in his coffee mug.

"Well, I have to get ready for work. Dump the dirty sheets in the laundry bucket; I'll put fresh ones on later when I get home."

Kim muttered something under her breath and set about fixing breakfast. Twenty minutes later, Doug and Angela were ready to head off to work.

"Kim, do me a favour and come home early again."

"Why? I was going to meet friends after school. We were going to go somewhere."

"Where?"

"Umm, a friend's place."

"Okay, but don't be late. You've got homework."

Angela kissed and hugged Kim while Doug waved goodbye, and together they left.

When they arrived at the station and clocked in, they considered going straight to Sergeant Wilmore and telling him their suspicions, but refrained from doing so. He seemed to be in a bad mood this morning as he barked everyone's orders for the day. Angela wanted to check on the house first, anyway. If Wilmore decided not to listen to them, the only option left would be go back and face Joe's spirit again, try and get him to reveal more details—something they could use as solid evidence.

They set out in the patrol car and headed straight to Parkland Drive, driving down slowly. There were a couple of maintenance men there; one pulling up the weeds, the other scraping off old paintwork. Angela glanced up at the bedroom windows, immediately feeling a prickle of unease on the back of her neck. Was Joe standing there right now watching them?

"Let's go turn around and act like inquisitive officers while I try the front door," said Angela.

Doug nodded and continued.

*Please let that door be open. Maybe there's another clue or something in there right now. Something we can use to arrest Hawthorn and let this nightmare be over. Before something other than a scratch appears on my daughter's body.*

*Maybe I should send Kim to stay with my mother for a while, should the unthinkable happen. If we don't get anything today, I think I'm going to have to.*

Doug turned around at the bottom of the cul-de-sac and returned up the road, stopping outside number 11. The two maintenance men glanced behind them and continued their work. She wondered if they knew the history of the place and if they would have been as willing to work here. Did either of them have kids?

"Anything wrong?" asked one of them, a rollup cigarette dangling from his mouth as Doug and Angela entered the garden.

"No, not at all. There was an incident here recently. Just checking for possible loiterers, breaking and entering," said Doug.

The guy with the rollup shrugged and continued scraping the old paint. "Place should be knocked down and rebuilt if you ask me. Gives me the creeps. Like no one has painted this place since it was built. Or bothered with the garden. Place looks derelict. Keep thinking I see shadows moving about in there, too. I got no idea why anyone would want to live in this piece of crap."

Angela's spine vibrated with icy unease, like a tuning fork. *Keep thinking I see shadows moving about in there.* Now that they were here, she was hesitant to try the front door. She didn't suppose these two would have a key. If the door was locked and there was no way inside…Angela had forgotten to bring her own spare.

She glanced at Doug as she reached for the door handle. The look of worry in his eyes reflected her own sentiment. She tried the handle.

It was locked.

*Oh no.*

She tried it again, but it refused to budge.

"Shit! I don't suppose either of you two got keys to the place?" she asked in desperation.

"Nope. We're not allowed in. We are just here to make a start on the outside, get it ready for the next family. Why they'd want to bring up a kid in a shithole like this I got no idea. Still, at least it'll be painted by the end of the week and the garden won't look like a jungle."

"Shit," muttered Doug. "This is not looking good. Let's try the back."

They left the garden and went around to the back of the house. It was the first time they'd seen the house from the back, and it looked just as bad as the front. Like a stain on an otherwise perfect picture postcard, its grimy, filthy windows and peeling paintwork a strong contrast to the other houses. As if the house itself was trying to shred the last remnants of a troubled past and start afresh. Or maybe it was the spirit of Joe Glazer—his rage seeping into the foundations of the house like a pollutant, affecting everything in its path.

They reached the back door and glanced at each other again. If it didn't open, there was always the option of heading to the agency and demanding keys, but this would put Hawthorn's guard up again and she didn't want that. She imagined once more standing over Kim while she slept, with a big knife in her hand, telling her that she had to do it, Joe was making her. That she was sorry, but she had no choice; her actions were not her own anymore.

The door opened.

Angela gasped in relief. She had been so convinced this door would be locked, too, that for a moment all she could do was stare at the gap as if hallucinating. A waft of air freshener greeted her as she opened it further and stepped in. She turned to Doug, who remained at the threshold, as if something prevented him from physically entering.

"Let's have a quick look around. Maybe Joe has left us more clues."

But Doug shook his head. "No, I'm sorry, but I'm not going in there. And I don't think you should either. It's dangerous."

"My daughter's life depends on it, Doug! We discussed this. We have nothing on Hawthorn. You saw Kim's arm. What if she didn't do it to herself? I'm already having weird nightmares where I see her injured or worse. It's started, Doug. Unless we catch him, Kim is going to be next."

She started sobbing.

"And that's why we need to speak to the Sarge. Tell him what Miles told us, show him the photo on your phone. They're trained better than we are. Maybe they can bring Hawthorn in, put pressure on him until he relents. Fuck, maybe even call his bluff, tell him they have evidence putting him at one of the crime scenes. Something related to DNA or technical advances."

In that split second she hated Doug, even though she knew he was right. If Joe hadn't given them more before it was because he was unable. What tangible evidence could he provide them with? Even if he spelled out Nickolas Hawthorn's name in full, what difference did it make? Without evidence they were fucked.

Reluctantly, on the verge of reaching out to Joe one last time, but deciding against it, she closed the door and dejectedly headed back to the car.

"Okay, let's go see Sergeant Wilmore. But if he laughs at us or throws us off the force, I'm coming back and not leaving until I have something on Hawthorn."

"Fine. Let's do it."

Sergeant Harry Wilmore's eyes widened when he saw them enter his office. There could be any number of reasons for coming back to the station, and Angela guessed he was considering all worst-case scenarios.

"What's happened?" he said in his gruff voice as she closed the door behind them. He was an imposing figure at the best of times, six foot five, well-built body, and his grey hair cut short military style. He was known for being impatient and rarely had a smile for anyone. His brown eyes glared at them, searching for a suggestion of what was to come.

Doug and Angela cast nervous glances at each other. Doug had no intention of saying anything—that much was clear, so Angela took a deep breath and began. For now, she avoided mentioning the spirit of Joe, only telling Wilmore that when she had returned to the house on her second visit, she had found the bloody word spelled out on the floor. Then she told him she had been doing her own investigation into both the serial killer case and the murders at Parkland Drive. She mentioned visiting Chris Miles and his eyes widened in apparent disbelief after she relayed what he'd told them and his suspicions about the agency owner.

"And you've been doing this while you're supposed to be on patrol?"

"Well, not really. Most of the time after our shift finished and our days off. I was only going back to the house to check kids weren't messing around there. Homeless people and drug addicts looking for somewhere to sleep."

Doug was looking sheepish, having apparently found something interesting on the floor to look at while Angela's heart pounded like a drum.

"You know I'm on personal terms with Hawthorn, don't you? We have done a lot of business together. We meet every Christmas for a drink. And now you're telling me he might be a serial killer from about thirty years ago? Based on a cryptic message you found and what a retired detective told you? A detective, I might add, who wasn't the most popular on the force. I worked with him back in the day just before he retired. He was suspected of being involved in a few cases of corruption and possible blackmail. So based on those two things, you want me to arrest Hawthorn or get the SCU to look into him?"

"Well, umm, Miles told us that Hawthorn said he went to the gym four times a week, but Miles discovered it was only twice, so he was hiding something. Our thinking was that being such a small village it had to be a local. Miles said they questioned everyone and considered the possibility that maybe the serial killer and these deaths at Parkland Drive were connected. Only the person renting out the house would know if they had daughters or not. Hawthorn had just started the letting agency at the time."

The Sarge leaned back in his chair, lacing giant, shovel-like hands behind his head and he studied the two officers. It was all Angela could do to maintain eye contact while she silently pleaded for him to say the magic words. *Okay, you've got a point. I'll reopen the case.*

"What's your interest in all this? It's obvious you've dragged your partner into it and you're calling the shots, because he hasn't said a word, so this is obviously something personal. What?"

It was all bubbling away behind her lips, the desire to blurt out everything, but she bit down on her tongue, forcing herself to think straight. He hadn't laughed, hadn't reprimanded them for not doing what they were paid to do, but seemed to be actually considering what she had to say.

"I need more," he said finally. "Before I can even consider reopening a cold case. And, I hasten to add, you're not paid to spend the day interviewing potential suspects or retired detectives. So I'm not going to ask you to bring me more evidence because it's not your job to do so, but I will mention it to Norwich Headquarters, who works on such cases. And if I find out you've spoken to either Miles or Hawthorn again, I'll have you on traffic duty the rest of the year. Now get back to work."

# Twenty-Two

Today was the day Kim, Chris and Lisa had planned on going to the house to see if it really was haunted or not, but when they had got there, there had been two men working outside on the house. Their disappointment had been huge—it was the last thing they had expected. Kim could barely contain her excitement as they made their way towards Parkland Drive, with Chris begging her for more information, suggesting what they do once inside and what to do if they saw or heard anything. And it had all been for nothing.

They had stood across the road looking into the upstairs windows, hoping for something to appear, something to reignite their lost excitement. But nothing moved. Except for the exterior, it looked like every other house in the cul-de-sac.

"We'll have to come back," said Chris. "When they're not here. That, or we wait for them to finish for the day."

That sounded like a better idea because Kim really didn't want to wait until the next weekend; she wanted to go in there now. Maintain the momentum with Chris. Afterwards they could go back to her house to discuss anything they might have seen, and if they hadn't they could make plans. But to wait until the workmen finished was not a viable option. Her mother had told her to come home early and she didn't want to disappoint her. Mum looked like she was about to explode at any moment, a bundle of nerves who jumped at the slightest sound. She made an excuse, that she had loads of homework to catch up on, and suggested they come Saturday. And of course, they could still plan on what they were going to do in the meantime. Kim told them she'd look at Mum's laptop again, see if there were any more juicy details. That worked well for Chris.

But now, as Kim lay sprawled on her bed, scrolling through Twitter, she felt empty again. The tug in her heart being near Chris had died down and all that remained were memories, his features buried into her subconscious the only thing she had to grasp onto until school tomorrow. They'd already texted each other for an hour earlier, but then he had to go to football training. It was going to feel like forever until tomorrow rolled around.

She thought of going to watch a movie with Mum, but she seemed constantly agitated lately. She'd caught her mumbling to herself, suddenly alert like a sleeping dog when she heard something outside. Maybe it was the stress of being a police officer; Kim had seen enough true crime documentaries to know police officers never truly switched off. Or maybe it was that house that was bothering her. She'd heard her and Doug chatting, conspiratorially, earlier, hand over her mouth so Kim wouldn't hear, but she'd caught the words *house*, *daughter* and *serial killer* a couple of times, so that had to be it. To Kim this wasn't a surprise; if she was a cop she'd probably do the exact same thing.

She turned on her TV and switched to Netflix, deciding to rewatch The Matrix because Keanu Reeves was gorgeous, and began to absently rub the itchy mark on her arm. It had seriously freaked her out when she woke up and saw the blood-stained blanket, then the scratch, thinking she had been bleeding to death at first. There was no way she had done that to herself, but given the other options, she'd had no choice but to assume she had. Now, rather than hurt, it itched like hell. She climbed into bed and pulled the blanket up. Kim was just ten minutes into the movie when the wardrobe doors suddenly opened by themselves.

It was cold and raining outside, so the window was closed. There was no reason for the doors to open, no draft or breeze that could have caught it. Groaning, she quickly jumped up, slammed them shut, and jumped back into bed. Before she'd even had the chance to pull the blanket up to her shoulders, they opened once more.

"What the hell?" she moaned.

She decided to leave it, too lazy to get up and close them again, but there was some horrid, musty smell coming from inside, as if she'd left dirty laundry in there for the last week. But it was something more than that, too. A coppery smell and...no, that wasn't the odour of smelly socks, it was much stronger. Similar to when she walked past the rubbish bins outside in the summer and they were filled not with just flies, but the stench of rotting meat. She covered her nostrils and mouth with her hand and went to check it out when she heard a noise coming from in there. A shuffling sound, like there was some small animal rustling through her stuff.

*Oh my God. There are rats in my wardrobe,* was her initial thought. But this seemed ridiculous—she'd never seen so much as a mouse in their home, and if there were rats she would have seen rat shit this morning when getting out clothes for school.

The rustling grew louder, so now it sounded like wind when the window was left slightly ajar. Whistling that creeped her out or...whispering. Was that whispering she was hearing in there? Her body felt as though it was shrinking, pulling the skin tighter like some kind of defence against infection. It was stiff, glued to the sheets, unable to move. Whatever she was hearing in there gradually took on a more focused aspect—she was sure she could hear her name being whispered from behind the jackets, jumpers, and dresses hanging up. It was so dark in there, but she was pretty sure she saw movement, a shadow moving among the others.

She glanced around her bedside table. There was her phone, a book she had been reading, and her lamp. She thought about screaming for mum, dashing out and getting her to see whatever it was and kill it—she was a cop, that was what cops did, investigate, but she wasn't sure her body would respond or that her vocal chords would react the way she wanted them to. Every part of her was paralysed, frozen in place, her heart wedged tightly in her throat and preventing any scream from forming.

Two glowing spots appeared like distant planets flickering like flames. They grew bigger until she could see the golden irises staring out at her. There was a dripping sound like a leaking tap, and when the thing stepped further out she saw it wasn't water dripping from it but something much thicker. "Kim," it hissed in a croaky voice. An arm reached out from inside the wardrobe, what remained of the skin leathery and black in places, bone poking through where chunks of flesh had fallen off. A gnarled finger pointed at her, wiggling back and forth as though scolding her. The hand suddenly curled into a fist, and before she knew what was happening she was thrown from the bed, landing heavily on the floor.

This should have been the moment for her to jump up and run screaming, but the only thing functioning was her bladder as a warm patch developed beneath her. Her brain seemed to have forgotten the idea of escape because all she could do was stare, wide-eyed and terrified, at the thing now halfway out of the wardrobe.

Most of its face was missing. Small lumps continued to fall to the floor as though it was shedding some foul skin yet taking with it all the flesh and bone as well. One bulbous, gelatinous eye glared at her while the other was sunken deep into its head. Drool, mixed with blood and other colourless secretions, ran constantly from what remained of its mouth.

It uncurled a finger and swiped at the air. Kim jerked violently and whimpered when she felt something warm and wet running down her cheek. As it dripped onto her pyjama top she noticed in her peripheral vision it was blood. Her cheek throbbed painfully. The thing swiped the air again, this time vertically and another stinging sensation pummelled her chest. Still unable to move, she glanced down to see a red patch appear just above her breasts, as though her thundering heart had finally pushed itself through the tight confines of her ribcage.

"Do it, Kim. Do it," it hissed. "Kill yourself or I'll do it for you. Slower. More painful. You choose."

Then it raised its arm again and slashed the cold air. Kim jerked violently and felt another sting to her forehead. Her vision became blurry, everything was foggy as though she was turning blind in that instant. Her eyes stung and it was only when she blinked and saw red she realised it was blood dripping into them. The thing turned and faded back into the wardrobe, the doors slamming shut behind it. It was then that Kim's body and brain finally found a connection to each other and she ran screaming downstairs to her mother.

## Twenty-Three

Fortunately, Kim's gashes on her face, cheek and chest weren't as deep as the amount of blood and hysterical screaming suggested, but even so, Angela took her to hospital to get them bandaged, fobbing off the doctor with a story about Kim being attacked by a stray dog. They'd given her a tetanus injection just in case, and they soon left.

Instead of taking Kim home, she took her to her mother's. Whether it would make a difference or not she didn't know, but she had to at least try. It had taken Kim ages to calm down, screaming about being thrown out of bed, a thing in the wardrobe with half its face missing that made the gashes miraculously appear, and the message it had left before it disappeared. Angela had burst into the room, despite Kim begging her not to, and had thrown open the wardrobe doors but there had been nothing there. Only the lingering stench of rot and decay. Joe was using Jimmy to get to Kim, just as she had suspected. It wouldn't be long now.

It was getting late and Kim pleaded and begged her not to leave, and Angela really didn't want to. She'd had to prise her trembling fingers from her, unwrap the arms that held on for dear life while Angela's mother looked on both shocked and horrified. Finally, against her better judgment, she had told her mum to give Kim one of her Valium pills to help her relax, and eventually Kim had succumbed to her immense fright, falling asleep on the sofa through sheer exhaustion.

Angela was sobbing as she got in her car. She'd been holding it back, trying to be strong for Kim, and not wanting her to see the utter terror in her face. Because now it was a question of priorities. And staying the night to console her terrified daughter, as much as she had wanted to, was not the first. There was no more time for that.

She thought of phoning Doug, asking him to accompany her, but she guessed that no matter how much he wanted to help and would do pretty much anything she asked of him, after seeing his face this morning in the back garden of 11 Parkland Drive, he would make an excuse and decline. There wasn't anything he could do to help her now, anyway. Not with what she had in mind.

She arrived at Parkland Drive and forced herself to drive slow, not bring any unwanted attention to herself. If neighbours were curious during the day, seeing her enter the house in the middle of the night would only exacerbate their curiosity. She parked at the top of the road to avoid unwanted attention and tried to walk as calmly as possible towards the house. The garden now resembled something other than a miniature rainforest and the flaking paint on the front wall had all been scraped away. It didn't do anything to take away the gloominess of the place, though, the grimy windows like the eyes of a giant, the cracks in the walls its skin shedding slowly and transforming into something much more terrifying and deadly. And within those walls was its host, lurking in the shadows, preparing to take its next victim.

Kim.

Angela glanced around the street, trying to appear as inconspicuous as possible, thankful it was late and most lights were off in the other houses. Confident no one was watching, she quickly walked to the back of the house. As she stepped into the garden, scanning the upper windows, the burden of what was needed threatened to overwhelm her. If Joe failed to respond, if he decided it was too late and things had already been set in motion, all that would be left would be to try and find an exorcist. She wasn't even sure such people existed outside of the movies. Especially in the small village churches that surrounded the area.

She opened the back door and stepped inside, not even sure if the place had electricity. She figured it must have if people were starting to work on the place. She'd brought a torch with her just in case. When she flicked the switch in the kitchen and no lights came on, she turned on the torch and shone it around, the beam casting monstrous shadows that didn't seem to belong to any feasible object.

It was cold inside, almost as cold as outside, and she could see weak streams of frigid air coming from her lips like ghosts as she breathed heavily. She closed the door behind her, shining the torch to look for the fuse box. Usually it was located at the front of the house, so slowly she headed towards the front door, her body rigid with fear and uncertainty, yet at the same time pure determination. She wasn't leaving this damn house until she had something to go on.

She found the fuse box and flicked all the switches. Nothing. Cursing she tried again, yet when no lights came on, no humming of fridge freezers, she resigned herself to having to rely on the torch. She shone it along the hallway towards the basement door that was now wide open. She was about to call out to Joe when there was a scratching noise behind her. She froze, not daring to turn around but knowing she had to confront him if he was here to threaten and torment her. Angela took a deep breath and slowly turned.

Two bright eyes glared at her through frosted glass at the foot of the door. She gasped in surprise and took a step back. Distorted by the glass they looked like glowing fireballs in the beam of the torch, never blinking, never wavering. Was it one of the dead trying to get in, warn her perhaps? Tell her it was too late and Kim was doomed? But then it scratched at the door again and meowed.

For a second she didn't recognise the distinct feline sound, guessing it to be an alien language spoken by the dead, until her brain made the connections, and she had to stifle a chuckle. Something grabbed the cat's attention and it bolted.

She turned around, ready to go down to the basement, and once again froze. At the far end of the hallway in the kitchen was a figure. A shadow in human form, completely black. When she shone her beam in its direction, it vanished. When she moved it away again it was a step closer in the side beam. She repeated the exercise. Each time she removed the torch's beam directly from the figure it was one step closer.

A loud thud came from upstairs, then the sound of something being dragged along the carpeted floor. A distant scream echoed around the house. The basement door creaked.

"Joe? Is that you? I know who did it, Joe. I can help find Suzy's killer but I need more. I need evidence. You don't have to hurt my Kim, I want to help you but I need more. Please."

A groan resounded, as though the foundations of the house itself were answering her. A cold draft rose from the floor, freezing her skin, goosebumps sprouting on her arms. Her teeth rattled like maracas. Something blew onto the back of her neck. She spun around, saw nothing, then when she turned back the shadow was mere inches from her face. A solid black form emanating a stench of foul, rotting matter that soured her nostrils and would have made her gag had her bodily functions not seized in horror.

Whoever or whatever it was, the featureless black phantom presence was gauging her, reading her mind. She could almost feel invisible hands wading through her memories, dragging up and sifting through her darkest, most tortuous memories, perhaps deciding whether she should live or die. Whether Kim should live or die. The thing growled, perhaps its idea of a chuckle, as it saw young Angela watching helplessly while her brother was killed and she did nothing. Jimmy returning in her nightmares, refusing to let her forget her traitorous actions. Her head throbbed on both sides, as though her brain was bouncing around her skull while those invisible hands searched for more.

The thing edged closer so now she could feel it on her skin. A blackness, as dark as the deepest mineshaft, that now possessed a solidity to it, pressing against her, as though she'd been coated in thick tar. There was movement where its mouth should have been and from it flew thousands of small bugs like moths or flies. They circled her head, a buzzing that threatened to drive her insane. Hundreds of them flew around her, circling her body as if searching for an entrance. She was going to open her mouth to scream, inadvertently permitting them access for whatever foul means they intended, and they flew off in unison and landed on the wall, squirming as one mass, each jostling for a better position.

The black form turned towards the insect things on the wall, as did Angela, her torch dangling from a hand that could barely grasp it any longer. As she watched, she realised there was a reason to their seemingly mindless actions. Shapes started to form on the wall, apparently random at first until she saw they weren't just haphazard, but letters. It was still hard to determine but they were spelling out that word again, NIKES. But she already knew this. She knew it must mean Nickolas Hawthorn, but she was hardly able to present this to Sergeant Wilmore as new evidence.

She wasn't as afraid as she had been; the thing was trying to help, had perhaps read in her mind that she was here to help, not hinder him. That finally there was someone here who could stop the hurt and rage he had been suffering all these years.

"It's not enough!" she cried. "I need solid evidence."

The moth-like creatures stopped when the letter S was formed.

"I know, Joe. Nikes. Nickolas. But give me something to incriminate him with."

A piercing howl caused her to trip over her feet in panic and crash to the ground. She screamed, her eardrums at straining point, ready to burst. The insects scattered, flying around the air, their wings and buzzing adding to the cacophony of hellish sounds. The whole house shook as the wailing continued, the basement door opening and slamming with such force the hinges came loose. Cracks appeared in the plasterwork where the insects had been, a series of jagged lines like scars. The sound of a police siren reverberated around the house, lights turned on of their own accord, yet instead of emitting a warm yellow glow they flashed blue. And then she thought she began to understand. She should have guessed earlier. It was so obvious now. It hadn't been the agency owner at all. It was trying to tell her it was someone else. Someone with a very similar name to the word spelled out on the wall and in blood in the basement. It hadn't been the letter N at all but a smudged M. And that changed everything.

"I know!" she yelled as loud as she could, the noise in the hallway as though she was standing next to a building being demolished. The insects flew incessantly around her, yet as soon as she yelled those words, they immediately began to fly back into the dark form's mouth. Abruptly, there was silence.

"I know who it is," she gasped. "I'll stop him, but please don't hurt my baby."

A rumble resounded around the house, like the empty stomach of a giant. An image flashed through her mind of Kim, lying in bed, a dark shape standing next to her, something long and glistening in its hand. Kim was pleading with it to just do it, finish it, she couldn't take anymore, and as the blade rose, the figure's head turned towards Angela and she saw herself looking back, her lips curled into a twisted grin just as the blade came down, and the image was gone.

When she looked up the figure had gone, too, as had all the insects. All that was visible were the monstrous shadows of a more mundane aspect that her torch picked up in the darkness. An amalgam of emotions threatened to cripple her. She believed she finally knew who was responsible for the death of Joe's daughter and all the others. Someone she suspected from the moment she set eyes upon him, yet who had also tricked her by pointing blame in a different direction, just as her emotionally wrought brain had misinterpreted the clues left by the vengeful spectre. Her emotions were also torn over Joe Glazer's spirit; a man who had been incapable of moving on following his daughter's death and for whom she should have felt great pity, yet he had done despicable things in the name of grief and revenge and she could never forgive him for that. She still wasn't entirely sure Kim was safe yet. Not until she made the arrest anyway, and that didn't seem as easy as she originally thought.

She felt a mixture of relief, anger and sadness that engulfed her as she slowly made her way out of the house again, fumbling in her pocket for her phone. It took several attempts but she finally found Doug's number and rang him.

"What is it? What's happened now? Do you know what time it is? Where are you?" he groaned.

"I'm at the house, Doug. I'm leaving now, in fact."

"What! What the fuck are you doing there again? On your own. Are you mad?" he almost yelled into her ear.

"It came for Kim, Doug. Attacked her. I had to take her to the hospital to get bandaged up. She's staying at my mother's for now, just in case. I was so angry. I left her there and came here, intent on demanding Joe to give us more answers."

"Jesus Chris, Angela. That's terrible, but even so, you in that house alone. Anything could have happened to you as well."

"It did happen, Doug. It did."

"What? What happened?"

She told him.

# Twenty-Four

When Kim woke up the next morning, there was a note beside her bed. It took a little while to remember where she was—her head was groggy and her body ached all over. Then she remembered what happened the night before and that her grandmother had given her a pill to help her calm down. She pushed herself slowly upright, wincing as the bandages pulled tight on her chest. She picked up the note—it was from her mother: *So sorry, honey, but something came up and had to leave for work early. Will phone later. I promise what happened last night won't happen again. I've fixed it. Stay at home today. Mum. XXX.*

Kim threw the letter away in disgust and slid back under the blanket. Now that she was starting to wake up properly, her mind returned to last night and what she had seen. It had to be impossible, surely. She'd had another nightmare, only this time so realistic she had somehow managed to cut herself repeatedly in the process. *Bullshit. I didn't dream or imagine that.* She peered inside her pyjama top and saw the bandage crossing her chest. Then she ran a hand across her face and, as if on cue, the tears began welling in her eyes. Through both fear and terror.

She recalled seeing that thing in the wardrobe, how it had smelled so gross, then hearing it, seeing it, being thrown from her bed, how it had stepped out, and by swishing the air magically made cuts appear on her face and chest.

She hadn't imagined it at all. That thing could have killed her if it had wanted to. Why it hadn't she didn't know, but right now she knew that thing in her wardrobe had been so real she already decided not to go back to that house again. She would stay here with her grandmother until her mother sold the place and bought another. And the idea it was somehow related to what her mother was investigating didn't go amiss on her, either. She'd heard her speaking to Doug about a presence in Parkland Drive, forcing people to kill their kids. Is that what was happening here? It said something before disappearing but she couldn't remember what it was. But as long as she stayed here with grandma, surely it wouldn't be able to get to her? Besides, that note said it wouldn't happen again—Mum must have done whatever was needed for it to stop.

There was the other issue, in its own way just as terrible. What if the gashes on her face left scars? Permanent scars. She'd look like a freak, that's what, and Chris would never go near her again, let alone look at her. It would be over. He'd probably try his luck with Lisa instead, even though she had a new boyfriend and she'd be alone forever, a victim with major facial disfigurements. Condemned to spend the rest of her life in solitude, people laughing at her behind her back; the freak that got attacked by a ghost, they would say; don't go near her in case it's contagious.

This fact alone was even more terrifying than what happened last night. That issue she had already decided was solved, but what about permanent disfiguration?

She turned on her phone and scrolled through photos of her and Chris together, laughing, pulling funny faces. Tears ran down her cheeks; now the funny face, at least with her, would be permanent. It was over, she might as well delete Chris and everyone else from her contacts list. Hell, she might as well throw away the phone.

*You're exaggerating. You didn't even need stitches. They were superficial wounds. Check for yourself.*

She was too scared to. Because what if they would leave scars? On her forehead, cheeks, chest. But she knew that if she didn't look the doubt would linger for weeks, and she knew she couldn't go that long without going mad.

Groaning, she staggered out of bed and hobbled to the wardrobe that had a long mirror embedded into the door. For a moment she felt a rising panic, certain something was about to burst out and attack her again. The only way to prevent it was to throw open the doors and check. Holding her breath, she turned half sideways, ready to bolt out the room if necessary, then reached out and touched the door handle. Her eyes squinting, almost afraid to look, she slung them open. There was nothing there.

She chuckled, feeling foolish, even though she had absolutely no reason to —the evidence was there for all to see if necessary. Kim closed them again and took off her pyjama top. She didn't really want to check the bandages on her face yet, in case she tore open the cuts, but she needed to look at her chest. Gritting her teeth, she slowly peeled off the plaster covering the bandage, wincing at the stinging of her skin. Last night she had been convinced she was bleeding to death, that the gashes must have been so deep they had struck bone, but now looking at her chest, it was barely a scratch. Like the one on her arm the other day that had almost healed.

Kim sobbed in relief as she replaced the bandage and looked at herself in the mirror. A plaster across her left cheek and another on her forehead. She reckoned she still looked like a freak, but thoughts of spending the rest of her life as a hermit, and shunned by all, thankfully vanished. It occurred to her she could use this to her advantage. They had gone to that house yesterday but had been stopped by the workmen, and after last night she decided she wasn't ever going near the damn place again. Besides, she planned on going into hiding until she could successfully cover the scars with makeup, but now, thinking about it, if she told Chris she had nearly been killed by the thing in her wardrobe and had the scars to prove it, what would he have to say to that? She thought she could guess the answer already.

He wouldn't see her scars as something horrific and ugly. After she told him he would see them as battle scars, something to be in awe of. She'd have to fight him off with a stick. But still, the idea of going near that house...

*Maybe he won't want to after seeing what happened to me. Maybe he'll just want to stand outside and hope to see something in the window.*

Yeah, that might be enough for him.

---

As expected, when Kim texted Chris and gave him a hint of what occurred, he had bombarded her with messages in between classes. They agreed to meet at Parkland Drive after school. It took some convincing for her grandmother to let her go out after pampering her all day, telling her she should stay home and rest, but when she insisted she had to meet Lisa to study for an important exam, she relented.

It was cold outside, so she put on a hoodie to help cover some of her face and made it to Parkland Drive without being noticed by anyone. On the way her mother phoned, but as always seemed distracted. She was at the police station and Kim could hear people talking in the background, so she quickly assured her mother she was okay and hung up. She arrived at the house to find Lisa and Chris already there.

"Shit, man. You weren't joking. What the fuck happened?" he asked, his eyes wide and a huge grin on his face.

She hugged Lisa, who looked more shocked than anything else. She told them what happened.

"I had to go to hospital, Lisa. I stayed at my grandmother's last night and I'm not going home ever again. At least until mum figures out whatever is going on and stops it. She left me a note this morning saying that was exactly what she was doing today."

"Shit," interrupted Chris. "It's to do with the house, ain't it. Must be. Your mum brought home the house's ghost; that's why it attacked you. Like those other kids that died in there."

"Yeah, I get the idea, Chris. I've never been so scared in my life."

"You're fucking brave if you ask me. I would have shit myself."

"I probably did," she replied, his words hitting her with the force of a speeding truck. *You're fucking brave if you ask me.*

"So we're going in, right?"

It felt like she had been hit by a lorry. Surely he didn't mean it, not after everything she'd just told them. He must have seen the look on their faces.

"C'mon. I mean there can't be anything in there now if it's at your place. Assuming they're connected. We just go in, have a quick look around, then leave. There's three of us, nothing will happen, but I wanna check anyway."

Kim turned to Lisa for moral support. She looked dubious, but also disinterested. Lisa didn't believe in ghosts.

"I don't mind. Might be a laugh."

*Shit.*

It had been raining for over an hour and was starting to fall harder. It explained why the workmen must have finished early.

She looked up at the windows, the rain running down the grimy glass, making it look like they were shedding black tears. If she said no, he might think differently of her, even though he had to understand she was scared after last night. But if he went in that house with Lisa, who knew what might happen between them. It would be their secret, and Chris would probably hang out with Lisa instead from now on.

"Alright, but let's be quick, and we don't split up."

It was only the beaming smile on his face and sparkling, gorgeous eyes that stopped her from throwing up with fear. Checking no one was watching, they hurried around the back of the house so no one would see them entering. When Chris opened the back door and they stepped in, the cuts on Kim's face and chest tingled and itched as if reminding her what she was getting into.

She had expected the place to be filthy, full of dust, the air hot and oppressive, perhaps spiders dangling from every corner, rats and bugs scurrying about. Here, on the inside, it looked like a perfectly normal house, nothing that suggested it was haunted. She absently scratched at the plasters on her cheek.

"Where'd they get murdered?" whispered Chris, as though there might be someone in here with them, or so the house itself didn't hear him.

"Everywhere, I think. In the bedrooms and down in the basement I think."

"Let's start upstairs, then."

They headed up the stairs, the only sounds their breathing and the occasional creaking of floorboards. Behind Kim's eyes was an image of that thing peering out from the wardrobe, its face dripping on the floor. At any second, she expected something to grab her from behind or throw her down the stairs. She was practically clutching the back of Chris's coat with both hands as they moved upstairs. The sense of being watched was overpowering. It was as if something was watching them from multiple angles at the same time, waiting for the right moment to pounce. She kept her focus on the back of Chris's green jacket, barely able to breathe.

They checked all the bedrooms, Lisa and Chris talking and giggling in hushed tones as they tried to imagine where the girls' bodies may have laid, Lisa quickly stepping to the side when Chris suggested she was probably standing where a huge pool of blood might have been. All Kim wanted to do was get out of here.

Then he said what she was dreading yet inevitably knew was coming.

"There's nothing here. Let's check the basement."

"Do we have to?" groaned Kim. "You said we'd be quick and there's nothing here. Not even any blood stains. Let's just go."

"Just the basement. Quick look and we're gone. Maybe they didn't clean up down there."

There was a strange gleam in Lisa's eyes, the suggestion of a smirk on her delicate features. Was she enjoying this? Knowing the only reason Kim dared to come in here was because she was infatuated with him? Maybe she wanted Chris for herself and had been lying about not being interested or having a boyfriend. Bitch.

With no choice but to follow, she left the last bedroom and went downstairs. Chris pointed to a small door by the stairs. It was open. Kim was pretty sure it hadn't been open when they'd walked past earlier.

"That must be the basement down there," whispered Chris.

They approached and peered down like three onlookers staring into some bottomless pit. None of them had thought to bring a torch. They were guided by the dismal light allowed to poke out from behind grey clouds and into grimy windows. Chris brought out his phone and switched on the light app. He shone it down onto the basement floor, waving it around creating eerie shadows. They began walking down the steps. Reluctantly, Kim followed after them.

The air was even hotter down here, stifling and thick. The sense of being watched was stronger, too. Every fibre in her body told her to get the hell out now. That thing in the wardrobe, whispering her name. At any second it was going to jump out from the shadows, drag her into a darkness so thick it would be like being sucked into a black hole.

"There's nothing down here, Chris. Let's g—"

The door to the basement slammed shut.

They all jumped and screamed simultaneously. Then Chris chuckled nervously, perhaps not wanting the girls to see he'd been genuinely spooked. He shone his beam up the stairs. Kim, now standing behind him, was surrounded by darkness. She could barely make out Lisa standing to her side.

"Must have been the wind or somethin'," said Chris, but it was clear from his tone he didn't really believe it.

"Oww, Kim. Get off, you're hurting me. Grab Chris, not me," said Lisa.

Kim turned to face her. She was standing a couple of metres to Kim's left. She wasn't touching her.

"Lisa," she said slowly, "I'm not touching you."

"Yes, you were. You just pulled my arm when the door slammed. And your hands are freezing!"

Chris, with his back to Kim, suddenly jerked as though he'd been pushed.

"What the fuck, Kim?" he said spinning around just in time to see Kim thrown across the basement and crash into the opposite wall.

Doug jumped in his car and raced to Angela's home. He felt like an idiot. He hadn't believed her about the ghostly sightings and had regretted jokingly suggesting she look into the agency owner as a possible suspect. She could have done something stupid if she tried to drag him into an investigation that wasn't theirs in the first place. She could have lost her job, they both could. Plus, the station being sued for harassment. Then from there, not only does she bring the retired detective into the game who feeds her false information about Hawthorn, her daughter Kim is...attacked? In her own home, thrown across the room and told she was going to die?

It was something out of a horror movie. These things didn't happen in real life. Sure, Bradwell had its own assortment of monsters, but these were locked up in Northgate. Human monsters, not things that crept out from wardrobes and attacked kids. Is that what happened to the other kids in that house? Tormented and threatened by some modern-day bogeyman? No wonder they begged their parents to be put out of their misery. And now, to top it all off, just when he thought Angela was going to go and arrest Hawthorn, or at least insist that someone from the SCU did, it turned out they were both wrong. This was why the serial killer had never been caught, and why Miles had made it his business to be the lead investigator into the Parkland Drive homicides. He must have been shocked, thinking there was a copycat. And of course, he would have interviewed those that worked at the agency, plus all the neighbours. The coincidences would have left him utterly stunned and confused. Had he made any connection to Joe committing suicide in that house and the subsequent homicides? Probably not. Miles hadn't come across as someone who might give things more than an afterthought.

And after Angela had told him this morning what she'd seen at the house last night, it had all made sense. The sirens, the flashing lights, the word NIKES that had been a simple misspelling. When they met this morning before their shift started, Angela wanted to go straight to Sergeant Wilmore. It had taken a lot of persuasion on his behalf to make her realise that they still didn't have any firm evidence incriminating anyone. If she so much as hinted at being in the house again, and what she had seen, Wilmore would not only have suspended her from duty, but insist she spend a week in Northgate, too.

*"Leave it with me,"* he had told her. *"Let me speak to someone I know in the SCU. See if they can dig anything up on Miles that might back our theory and warrant it being reopened."* She had agreed, but he only had until tonight. Kim's life depended upon it.

And now he had it.

When it was clear that Miles and his task force were getting nowhere and the village was in uproar, a separate group of detectives had carried out their own investigation. They had all agreed it had to be a local man carrying out the crimes and no way the perpetrator should not have been caught yet. According to Doug's source, a detective who was now retired, the separate task force had come to the conclusion that the reason the killer hadn't been caught was because it was someone who knew every piece of information they had, knew every step they were taking, and was always one step ahead of them.

A cop.

When Miles was always off duty when another body was found, suspicions were raised. He was monitored and followed, his phone tapped, yet whenever a fresh victim was taken, he had 'disappeared' from those tailing him. Many were convinced Miles was the killer. While he was at the station one day, detectives had broken into his home and found a piece of jewellery—a child's necklace—in one of his drawers. He had been brought in and questioned, but could not be arrested because it had been an illegal search.

Miles was released and invited to take an early retirement, which he did.

They had him. With the word NIKES now known to mean MILES, thanks to the smudges, they could get Sergeant Wilmore to reopen the case and pressure Miles into admitting his involvement. Angela was going to cry with delight.

He reached a crossroads and stopped at the red light. He realised Angela wasn't at home and banged the driving wheel with both hands; she was staying at her mother's place and where the hell was that? He searched his pockets for his phone, the seats next to and behind him. In his haste, he must have left it at home.

"Shit, shit, shit!"

*Think, Doug. Where would she be right now?*

He glanced at the car's clock—5:30. Kim wouldn't have gone to school today which meant she'd be at her grandmother's. Surely Angela would go straight home, that's what she said she was going to do, although before leaving she had phoned Kim to say she had a couple of things to do and would be back soon. What couple of things did she have to do?

Behind him a car beeped. He looked up to see the lights had turned green. He had a split-second decision to make. Could she still be at the house? Looking for one final piece of evidence, just in case?

"Fuck it." He turned right and headed towards Parkland Drive, praying she wasn't doing anything stupid.

He drove slowly down the cul-de-sac and was surprised not to see Angela's car parked anywhere. He reached the bottom, turned around and drove slowly back, unsure what to do. But just as he was about to give up, go home and phone her, he saw movement in the upstairs window of number 11.

"What the fuck is this? You are kidding me. Angela, don't tell me you brought your kid here. Are you fucking *mad* or what?" he yelled.

Upstairs, watching him from the bedroom window was Kim.

"Fuck, Angela. You got a death wish or something?"

He stopped the car and jumped out. Remembering the front door was locked he went around the back, his head already aching with anger and everything he planned on saying to her. He stormed down the garden path and threw the back door open.

"Angela, where the fuck are you? Get outta here now!"

He looked around wildly, straining to hear any noise that might be Angela or Kim. But it was deathly quiet.

"Angela? Kim? Come out, it's me, Doug!"

He thought he caught muffled giggling coming from somewhere, but it was hard to pinpoint. He'd seen Kim upstairs, so assumed she must be still up there, surely Angela wouldn't be so stupid as to leave her alone here. Realising where he was—as if it had only just occurred to him— made his skin prickle and muscles tighten.

"Oh, shit."

He then realised it wasn't the first time he had seen someone in an upstairs window. What if it wasn't Kim at all? What if...

He was about to turn and run from the house when he heard muffled sounds coming from near the front door. What might have been someone yelling. A voice, disturbingly similar to Kim's high-pitched squeak.

"Kim, is that you?"

The basement door shook on its hinges. What were they doing down there? Were they both trying to contact Joe? It was possible. He moved closer to the door, his body turned slightly, as though subconsciously preparing itself to bolt for the back door should it be necessary. He heard muffled giggling down there now, more high-pitched laughter.

"Kim? Angela? Is that you? Answer for God's sake!"

The door rattled again, as if someone was leaning against it. And then it slowly swung open. Doug waited, expecting Kim and her mother to step out into the hallway, big smiles on their faces now that it was all over, but instead nothing came out. Bewildered, he walked up to the door and poked his head around the corner, then peered down into the basement.

It was pitch black down there. Like staring into a cave. Nothing moved, no sounds came. He might have been staring off into space, a black void that continued for millions of miles.

"Angela?" he hissed, as if afraid to awaken or disturb something nefarious. He cursed himself for not bringing his phone with him so he could use the light. He cursed again when he realised his torch was in the car. There was no way he was going to go get it and come back. He considered leaving anyway, he didn't like this. But just as his mind was making the decision to leave he heard another faint chuckle coming from the bowels of the basement. He stepped closer, peering down the steps, looking for the source. He saw movement. Something shifted in the impenetrable darkness.

"Angela, is that you? Get out of there, for God's sake. It's me, Doug."

Then he heard a noise behind him. He spun around. And just had time to see the large, shadowy figure looming over him, two eyes like glowing embers staring down at him before he was roughly pushed down the stairs.

He flew through the air, missing the first set of steps, until his back collided with the bottom ones and a loud crack resonated around the room. Then a thump as his head hit the concrete floor. His breath was snatched from his lungs, the view ahead, up the stairs, was grey, large black spots dancing before his eyes. Grey except for the figure slowly gliding towards him. Stunned, his natural instincts kicked in as he tried to push himself away from the oncoming figure, but for some reason his scrambling hands failed to propel him. Everything beneath his neck was as though a separate part of him, detached from the rest. His eyes caught movement to his left. Someone was down here, yet his panic-stricken brain assumed it was another of the ghostly shadows coming for him. He tried to scream yet could only manage a whimper as his throat clogged with something warm and wet.

The figure reached the bottom of the steps and stood over him, translucent, shimmering, its eyes flames in a roaring fire. The figure squatted or diminished in size, as now its eyes were mere inches from his own, a stench coming from it like burning flesh. Doug just had time to hear a high-pitched scream and see Kim dash past him, screaming hysterically as she ran up the stairs before something dark and cold covered his face and eyes and very soon the whole world went black as his last breath was spluttered.

# Twenty-Five

Angela paced around her mother's house, not knowing what to do. She'd tried Doug's phone a dozen times already and all she got was a generic recording telling her to leave a message. Her daughter's phone was exactly the same, as if they'd got together and made a pact; let's make Mum's life even harder and more stressful by not answering our phones. That Kim had left the house was bad enough; after what the poor girl had been through, Angela couldn't fathom why she would want to leave ever again. She had to be in a state of extreme shock. When her mother said Kim had already arranged to study for an exam with a friend, she knew that was a damn lie. There was no way in hell that girl was in any condition to study for some exam. Angela had been on the brink of giving her mother a serious piece of her mind, but of course the woman hadn't known exactly what had occurred the night before—she still believed it had been a dog that attacked Kim.

So where the hell was she?

Where was Doug?

She had left a note for Kim this morning promising it would be all over, that she had what she needed to put a stop to this once and for all, and it had only been Doug's insistence that stopped her from bursting into Sergeant Wilmore's office or making a direct beeline for that fucker Miles' place. And now he'd disappeared as well.

*Maybe Kim went home. Maybe she went with friends to check if that thing was still there, perhaps trying to convince herself she had imagined it. Now, in the cold light of day, maybe she wanted to prove to herself and her friends that it hadn't been real.*

That was a very real possibility. She knew there was a kid she had a crush on and Kim had mentioned he loved all things supernatural and morbid true crime stuff on Netflix. The more she thought about it, the more Angela figured it was very likely Kim had phoned to tell him about what happened and they had gone together on a little ghost-hunting exercise.

"You idiot, Kim. You stupid idiot," she muttered.

"I'm going home, to see if Kim is there," she said to her panic-stricken mother. "If she comes back, tell her to phone me immediately. Or you phone me to tell me where she is."

"Okay. I'm sorry. I didn't know. I—"

"It's alright. Forget it."

Angela grabbed her car keys and quickly left.

When she arrived home, she stood for a moment in the garden, looking up at the bedroom windows, waiting to see if there was any movement—spectral or not. Seeing nothing move, no twitching curtains, she cautiously opened the front door and stepped inside.

She didn't know if it was her heightened state of anxiety, unable to shake off the idea that something bad had happened, but the house felt wrong as she wandered around downstairs looking for signs of Kim. There was an electrical charge to the air making the hair on the back of her neck prickle, her fingertips to tingle whenever she touched anything. It was as if the house itself was watching her every move, eyes everywhere burning into her head. That sixth sense that she possessed warned her something terrible was imminent or had already occurred; it filled her body and spirit with a dark foreboding, a sense of dread that almost made her puke.

"Kim!" she yelled, barely managing to utter the word. Her throat was clogged.

Hearing no reply, she headed upstairs. She would prefer never to enter Kim's bedroom again, just pack up and get the hell out of Bradwell with all its accursed hospitals and haunted houses, but the problem was solved, dammit—all they had to do was arrest Miles, force him to confess if necessary and this would be over. They were so close.

Hesitant, she opened Kim's bedroom, on the one hand fearful of being attacked, on the other hoping and praying Kim was in there with Chris as she replayed to him what happened last night. But it was empty. Clothes were strewn everywhere, splashes of blood on the walls and floor where Kim had been attacked, everything exactly as they had left it when they ran from the house. She wasn't here so where the fuck had she gone?

She turned to head out of the room, her phone in her hand ready to dial both Kim and Doug again when she heard a noise as she was closing the door. A creaking sound, and it certainly wasn't coming from the hinges on the bedroom door. She froze mid step, a blanket of unease wrapping itself around her cold body. A gust of foul air blew lazily her way, swirling above her, so thick she could taste and see it. There was a thud behind her, a heavy footstep. Another. Not wanting to but having no choice, she turned around to see Jimmy standing there, now barely more than a skeleton, just odd lumps of his grey flesh remaining on his body. The side of his face that had been more or less human was gone now, too, parts of his skull showing through while the rest resembled a squashed watermelon, bits dripping onto the floor, the top of his head now bald and cracked in places.

A skeletal arm reached out, fingers gnarled like the crooked limbs of trees. A sound came from his mouth, garbled as though filled with liquid, spraying bits of bone and flesh at her. She couldn't understand what he was saying, but she didn't need to; she could hear him in her head. *It's too late. Kim is dead. You should have helped me. Now you will suffer all eternity just as I do. You brought it all on yourself. Let me make it easier for you.* His other arm reached out, ready to embrace her, to drag her back to whatever foul realm he came from.

Rather than turn and run, she found her legs edging towards him of their own free will. Kim was dead. It was over. What did it matter anymore? Nothing mattered. Whether she arrested Miles or not wouldn't change the one single thing that she promised to do and had failed to protect her loved ones. Joe had got to Kim and she was probably lying in a pool of her own blood somewhere while her soul remained trapped in the darkest realms of hell. Better to give up now; at least this way she could repay her dead brother by offering her soul to him. Maybe in hell she could apologise to her daughter too. Tell her she had done her best, but of course her best had never been good enough.

She was within inches of those skeletal fingers, feeling the iciness emanating from them. She closed her eyes, ready to let her beloved little brother wrap them around her neck and squeeze the life from her when something made her jerk. A loud bang, someone screaming. Her eyes shot open and she recoiled, stepping backwards and almost tripping over her feet.

"Mum! Mum! Are you here? Help!"

Kim.

A howl shook the house. The gaping hole that was Jimmy's mouth widened, splitting the muscles that bound his jaws together. Angela ran from the room just as Jimmy swiped at her. She dashed down the stairs. Kim stood there, blood running down her cheeks and forehead from the reopened gashes on her face. Angela nearly sent them both crashing to the floor as she grabbed and hugged her, both with tears streaming down their faces. Another howl tore through their home, the walls shaking, paint flaking from cracked plasterboard. Angela grabbed Kim's arm and dragged her outside and said nothing until they were on the street.

"Where were you? Oh my God, I thought you were fucking dead! Jimmy said you were dead, where the fuck were you?" babbled Angela.

"It got us. Me, Chris and Lisa, but we managed to escape, but then Doug came and it killed him. It killed Doug!" wailed Kim.

"Whadaya mean got you? Who? Where?"

"The house. That thing that attacked me. In that house. It's my fault I took them there but then Doug came in and something pushed him down the stairs and he broke his neck and we got up and ran," she howled.

What was she talking about? The house got them? Doug? The thing? And then it dawned on her what house she was talking about.

"The house where the murders happened? What the hell were you doing there? What do you mean Doug? He went with you?"

"Mum, he's dead!"

She stared at her daughter, still gripping her arm tightly. Now even tighter, looking for answers in the girl's terrified eyes, she searched them like looking for clues to an eternal mystery. It didn't make sense. Doug was supposed to be coming here, with his latest piece of evidence to incriminate Miles; the earth-shattering revelation that was going to put a stop to all this, and now he was at the house? The house he refused to step in again? Why was he there?

"Mum!" insisted Kim, bawling her eyes out as she hugged her mother.

It jerked Angela from her shock. He was dead, Kim just said. Lying at the bottom of the steps in the basement with a broken neck. But that was impossible because this was over and…she saw Jimmy's face again in her mind, telling her it was too late, that she should give herself over to him as penitence for failing to save him all those years ago. Then she looked at Kim, the blood on her face now smearing Angela's jacket.

"Oh my God. Get in the car. Now!"

They both ran to the car and dived in. The engine roared to life and Angela sped off towards Parkland Drive. She could barely see where she was going as she floored the accelerator, attracting the wrath of fellow drivers and pedestrians as she flew through red lights and past zebra crossings without stopping. Surely Kim was lying or mistaken. It had to be another trick by Joe, perhaps to get her back to the house, because Doug had refused to enter last time; why would he go back there again on his own, without warning her of his intentions? Especially when he'd phoned her earlier to say he finally had what they needed?

"You're sure it was Doug? And what were you doing in there anyway?"

"It's all my fault!" wailed Kim. "I wanted to impress Chris by telling him the house was haunted, and he wanted to go inside, but after last night I didn't, but we went there anyway, and he kept insisting so I said we just have a quick look around and…and then we went to the basement and the door slammed shut. We were locked in then something threw me across the room and Doug came in. Something pushed him down the stairs and we ran. I heard his neck or something break when he hit the floor, but we ran," she babbled between sobs. "I didn't want to go in but Chris insisted and now…"

Kim covered her face with her arms and sobbed.

Fuck. This was her own fault. She suspected Kim had been looking through her laptop that night; she should have warned her about the house, told her the truth about what was happening, not lie to the girl and treat her like a child, as if hiding things might save her. She'd let down Jimmy, and now she was on the verge of doing the same to her daughter.

They arrived at Parkland Drive and Angela screeched to a halt. "Stay here! You understand? Do not move."

Kim nodded and said nothing. Angela jumped out and ran around the back of the house. The back door was open. She ran inside and headed straight to the basement; the door was wide open. Utter dark greeted, her yet she ignored the possibilities and gripped the handrail as she went down, pulling out her phone with her other hand. As soon as she turned the light on, she gasped and practically jumped to the floor.

"Oh fuck. Doug? Doug, can you hear me?"

But she knew the answer already. His face was bloated and swollen, purple tongue dangling from an open mouth as he looked up at her with dead, grey eyes like a shark's. She checked for a pulse anyway, and when it was confirmed he was dead, she burst into tears.

"Oh, Doug. I am so sorry! You should never have got caught up in all this. It's all my fault. Again."

As she stared into his lifeless eyes, a rage began to well inside her. He didn't have to die, he had nothing to do with this. Fuck, he was trying to help Joe, so why did he kill him?

"You bastard, Joe! You senseless bastard! He had the information I needed to arrest Miles and you killed him. Why? Don't you want Miles held accountable? Why did you do this, you heartless bastard?"

But no answer came. Nothing stirred, nothing moved in the shadows. Her immediate thought was do nothing, let Joe rot in his own filth, trapped between worlds forever, in permanent grief, but to do so would condemn Kim as well, and that was not going to happen. Too many innocent people had died already. She was about to call it in, perhaps anonymously for now, to give her time to think, when she noticed a piece of paper in the inside pocket of Doug's jacket. She pulled it out and read through it. It was a report torn from a file back at the station with a photo of Chris Miles on it and a detective's suspicions about his involvement in the case. She slumped onto the floor beside Doug. They suspected Miles all along. He had been their number one suspect but they had been unable to prove it.

*Oh, Doug. Why didn't you come straight to mine instead of coming here? What possessed you to do so?*

But possessed was the key word, because what if his intentions had been to go to Angela's all the time but had somehow got side-tracked? Deliberately perhaps? It was then she noticed the missed calls on her phone. As she flicked through them the majority came from Doug. He had tried calling her, but for some reason she hadn't heard them. And so he'd come here looking for her?

"You selfish bastard, Joe! I'm going to stop this now, but I'm doing this for me, not for you. I hope you rot in hell!"

She leaned over and kissed Doug's cheek, then stood up and left, grim determination her overriding emotion. Just as she stepped outside into the back garden and turned to close the door, a tall dark shadow watched her from the kitchen.

"Fuck you, Joe. Fuck you."

# Twenty-Six

On the way to her mother's house, Angela stopped at a payphone and called the police station informing them they should go to 11 Parkland Drive and would find a body in the basement. She did so anonymously, which made her feel like a common criminal, but the idea of leaving Doug to rot down there until she finished devising her plan was just as heart-breaking. If she informed them through official channels, she would very probably not get to fulfil her promise of bringing Miles to justice and it would all be over. She would accept whatever consequences came afterwards, but not before.

When they reached her mother's, she told Kim to go inside and stay there until she returned, which might be some time. Before Kim left the car, Angela explained a little of what she knew, who was responsible for what was happening to them and why, and Kim said nothing as she listened. Angela hugged her, kissed her forehead, and watched her walk down the garden path to her grandmother's.

"Will I ever see you again outside of a prison cell?" she wondered aloud. They might accuse her of having something to do with Doug's death, which in a way she did, but not the way they were thinking. Teary-eyed, she drove off to see Chris Miles.

She wasn't entirely sure what she was going to say to him, had no prepared speech in mind for when she confronted the creepy, sick individual, but she hoped she would be able to trick or manipulate him into revealing something or even confessing. Which she doubted. This man would not have lost a single night's sleep in all these years regarding what he'd done and the repercussions since. He was old now, so it was highly unlikely he was going to start feeling remorseful at this stage. But, with Doug's bloated dead face still prominent in her mind, the gashes cut into her daughter's face, the sight of Jimmy enticing her into giving up, she thought she'd beat a fucking confession out of him if necessary. She wasn't leaving without one. With the report Doug had taken from the original files in her pocket, she arrived at Miles' home and parked slightly further up the road so as not to alert him to her presence and thus give him time to prepare himself.

She locked her car and strolled purposefully towards his home. There was a light on in the living room, which she had expected. She walked down the garden path, his garden reminiscent of the one on Parkland Drive, weeds thick and tall, what little grass there was brown and in little patches. His windows were almost as dirty as the other house, too. She knocked on the door, her heart banging against her ribcage, yet too angry and filled with rage to be nervous. When she tried to fake a smile in preparation for him opening the door, she was only slightly surprised to realise her jaw ached—she had been grinding her teeth the whole journey.

The door opened only the tiniest bit and a familiar face peered out, a scowl permanently etched onto the old man's face.

"What?" he growled.

"Mr Miles, I'm Detective Harford. We spoke a few days ago. I have some more questions I'd like to ask you."

She had been on the verge of saying her and Doug but a sob had caught in her throat at the thought of him. It was imperative he let her in.

He grunted. "I told you everything I know. Why can't you let me rest in peace? I got nothing else to say."

He made to close the door but Angela stuck her foot between the door and the frame.

"We have new evidence that I'd like to discuss with you. Perhaps refresh your memory on certain things."

He stood staring at her, his eyes narrowed as if contemplating his best course of action. Her bones froze as he stared her up and down; is that the look the kids saw as he raped them before killing them? The last thing they ever saw was that chilling, evil glare while their lives were taken from them? He was a monster, disguised as a feeble old man. There was nothing feeble about him, though, she knew it. As feeble as the devil. And when he had been young and strong, perhaps he had been the devil himself, or an accurate representation of the fallen angel. What horror those poor kids had gone through.

"I told you, I don't remember nothin' anymore. Or you found somethin' on that Hawthorn?"

"It's possible," she said, hoping this would gain his attention.

"Well, if that's the case, all right, but make it quick. It's gettin' late and I'm tired."

Inwards, Angela grinned. *Tired? You don't know the meaning of the word.*

She stepped in, greeted by that musty odour of mildew and rank nicotine again. Miles shuffled towards the living room, his filthy white vest and old, tattered slippers making him appear as a poor, lonely old man. Angela kept the vision of Doug's grey, dead eyes looking up at her firmly fixed in her mind so as not to fall for his tricks and deceit.

He fell rather than sat in what was obviously his favourite

armchair, his cat immediately jumping onto his lap. He stroked it absently while lighting another cigarette, never taking his eyes off Angela. She felt like she was going to puke at any moment. Did he see through her disguise as detective in a serial killer case? He might be a lot of things, but he wasn't stupid.

"So what've you got?"

She pulled out the piece of paper from her jacket as she took a seat uninvited. If he thought she was going to just stand there like a little girl in front of the headmaster, he was wrong.

"I did some more investigating into the agency owner. Seems you were right, he wasn't going to the gym at all—he had a mistress. And he couldn't account for his whereabouts when several of the girls went missing, either."

"See, I told you. I knew it was him all along, just couldn't prove it. You gonna arrest him?"

"The team is still looking for more than just circumstantial evidence to tie him in. He didn't say anything else to you? His attitude towards the victims or the killer himself?"

"He acted like he wasn't that interested. Callous, if you ask me. Nasty piece of work. You take him in, tell him what you know and watch him crumble. You'll see. Good to hear after all these years—I can finally sleep peacefully at night without that burden."

Angela was sure she was talking to the most vile, despicable human being she had ever set eyes on. He was quite happy to incriminate an innocent man while speaking of sleeping peacefully at night. There was even the beginnings of a grin on his face—as best as he could manage, anyway. She was about to tell him the truth when he dragged himself to his feet.

"You want a coffee, something stronger? I feel like we've earned it."

What she wanted was to puke right there on his stained, brown carpet, then arrest him while slapping that sick little grin from his face, but instead, knowing it would take the old man a while to make it, she agreed to a coffee. It gave her an idea.

Miles shuffled off to the kitchen, at the opposite end of the house. She could hear him opening cupboards out of her line of sight, which was perfect. Not wasting any time, she began rummaging through drawers in an old cabinet by the window. As expected, they were full of useless crap and papers, hoarded over years and forgotten about. The amount of dust attested to the fact. Finding nothing, she squatted and checked the larger drawers at the bottom. Again, nothing.

"Shit," she hissed, an ear cocked towards the kitchen. The kettle was starting to whistle. Two more minutes until he'd be back and she'd have to confront him outright and hope for the best.

Next to his armchair was a smaller coffee table with two small drawers underneath it. A cold chill rippled up her spine, a slight dizzy spell which almost caused her to fall over. Her hands were shaking. Quickly, knowing what the sensation meant, she pulled open the drawers. It was full of papers again. Desperate and confused, she shuffled them looking underneath and that was when her heart leapt to her throat. Glittering under the papers were a number of small, fine pieces of jewellery. She grabbed them and held them up to the light. There were two silver necklaces and a gold one with the initials CT delicately swinging back and forth. The Tennant's daughter was called Carla.

"Here we go. I know you don't drink on duty—shouldn't do anyway—but a little drop of brandy never hurt anyone."

Miles entered slowly and carefully, concentrating on not spilling the two steaming mugs of coffee in his hands. Angela just had time to stuff the jewellery in her pocket before he handed her a mug.

"Cheers," he said and offered a smile that showed yellow, stained teeth. She thought of throwing the coffee in his face.

While Miles sat down, Angela had to do the same. Her hands were shaking so badly there was a risk of spilling her coffee not over Miles, but herself. Her legs threatened to betray her, her heart throbbed in her throat. She put the mug on the small coffee table beside her.

"Spent years wonderin' if I'd missed anything," he said. "There had to be somethin' linkin' him to those murders but hell, better late than never. You did a good job, you should be proud."

She couldn't take any more. She saw Doug, Kim, the Tennants in utter grief, the empty shell of Wanda in Northgate, Jimmy beckoning her with skeletal fingers.

"There was a separate investigation as well as your task force, did you know?"

His eyes squinted. He took a drag on his cigarette and spluttered. Angela had the certainty that he knew she wasn't a detective. Not just because the other day she had been in police uniform and now she was in plain clothes, either. Maybe this was all a show; the coffee, the insane grin, hoping to try and sound genuinely impressed with catching Hawthorn.

"Yeah, I know," he said finally. "Bunch of wasters, too. No good for shit. Waste of time and money."

"I read their report."

His hands appeared to be trembling more than usual. He had to hold his mug with both of them to stop coffee splashing onto himself.

"You know what I mean, then. They had no idea what they were doing. They even suspected someone on the force, can you believe that?"

This was it. She'd had enough. It was getting dark outside and she didn't think another night alone with Kim was one they were going to survive. Joe had already proven so.

"Yes, I can believe it. In fact, the reason I can believe it so much is because I know it's true. It was you, wasn't it? Not

Hawthorn, you were just trying to incriminate him, so your sick, vile, nasty little mind could relax. That's how you were going to sleep peacefully at night. Not because the killer was caught but because you'd managed to pin it on someone else. You are an evil, despicable monster for what you did and you are going to spend the rest of your miserable life in Northgate. And I hope from there you go on to rot in hell."

Miles eyes widened in fury, his lips curled up into a sneer, making him look more like the monster he was. His face was bright red, veins throbbing in his neck.

"Get out of my house," he growled.

A finger of fear gripped Angela's spine. Despite being an old man, she was sure he still retained enough strength in those skinny arms of his. But she hadn't come all this way to be dismissed so easily. She pulled the pieces of jewellery out of her pocket.

"Recognise these, Miles? Or more importantly, do you think their owners would recognise them? This one here could belong to the Tennant's daughter, Carla. My partner Doug died today, Miles. You know that? He died because of you. One of the girls you killed, Suzy Glazer? It's her father haunting Parkland Drive, making the parents kill their daughters and he won't stop until Suzy's killer is caught. So you're responsible for those murders, too. My daughter nearly died because of you. But now it's over."

Angela half expected it, but even so she was still caught unawares when in a surprising burst of speed from the old man, he dashed across the room and pushed her to the floor. She gasped, seeing stars as her head collided with the carpet hard enough to make it throb. She tried to push herself to her feet, but he was already kicking her in the stomach with what felt like boots rather than slippers. If she remained as she was in this defensive position he was going to kill her, of that she had no doubt, so, despite the repeated stamps on her head, she grabbed a leg with both hands and bit into the soft tissue of his calf as hard as she could.

Blood splattered into her mouth as Miles screamed, desperately trying to remove his foot by bending over and punching her in the face. At the same time, Miles was frantically looking around for something harder to hit her with, a heavy-looking glass ashtray was just out of reach. Angela tried to find something to fight him off with while her teeth were still firmly clamped around his calf. Miles tried to stamp on her head with his other foot and lost his balance causing him to stumble back and trip. Seeing her chance, Angela released her jaw, spitting out blood and bits of skin from her mouth and grabbed her coffee mug. She threw the steaming contents into his face, causing him to howl and clutch his face.

Fortunately, she had enough foresight to bring a set of handcuffs with her, so grabbed them from inside her jacket and rolled Miles onto his back. She had only managed to get one hand behind his back when the other swung back and caught her jaw. She stumbled, dropping the handcuffs, then, impossibly quick for a man of his age, he pushed himself up. His face was red and raw now, as were his eyes, making him look even more like the devil than before. He grabbed the empty mug and struck her over the head with it, smashing it instantly.

Her vision was blurring, the room around her grey and shimmery, to the point she thought it could be Jimmy or Joe stood over the other side of the room, but when Miles spat and cursed before charging at her with the glass ashtray she knew who it was and what was about to happen. The ashtray came crashing down towards her skull. Using what little strength remained, she rolled over just in time to hear a loud thud on the carpet. She grabbed his injured ankle and bit once more into the bleeding calf muscle. Miles howled, raising the ashtray once more, but this time Angela, the last of her adrenaline fading rapidly, managed to grasp a piece of the broken mug and stab it into his groin, reaching just far enough to make impact.

Miles dropped the ashtray, his face a mask of agony as he slowly crumbled to the floor, a large chunk of the mug still embedded in his crotch. Angela staggered to her feet, almost collapsing as blood trickled into her eyes, and wildly searched for her handcuffs, and seeing them half underneath Miles, she pulled them out and bound Miles' hands together as they clutched at his bleeding groin.

"I should let you bleed to death you piece of shit, but that would be too good for you. I want to see you spend the rest of your life with all the other sick, evil monsters in Northgate. Maybe the ghosts of those you killed will come and visit you just as they did me."

She pulled out her phone and dialled the station, then sat on the sofa and watched him squirm and writhe and whimper in agony. While she waited for the police and ambulance to arrive, she phoned Kim. The girl was scared, but when Angela assured her it was all over she sobbed, begging for Angela to come home.

"In a while, sweetheart. I have questions to answer first, but I'll be home soon. Love you," she said and hung up.

A few seconds later she heard the sirens, momentarily mistaking the noise for what she'd heard in the basement.

"Happy now, Joe?" she yelled. "Can you leave us alone now you've got what you wanted?"

No sound came. Instead, someone banging on the front door so she went to answer it. Three detectives stood there, shock and bewilderment on their faces as they took in the blood dripping down the side of her face and the mess in the living room. Miles groaned and tried to ask for help, but could only mutter incoherencies.

"He's in there," she said. "Miles. The uncaptured serial killer from all those years ago. In that drawer over there are pieces of jewellery he took from the victims. Kept them as trophies, the sick son of a bitch. These, too," she said holding up what she assumed to be Carla Tennant's necklace, plus the other two. One of the detective's rushed in when he saw Miles' body lying on the floor, blood gushing from his groin. The others, who Angela didn't know, still remained perplexed, perhaps wondering how and why a uniformed officer had managed to solve this long-standing cold case.

"I was investigating the case in my spare time," she said. "The Chief Inspector knows we suspected Miles; we just needed proof. And I found it."

The sound of more sirens broke the quiet as an ambulance screeched to a halt outside.

"Did you have a search warrant?" asked one of the detectives.

"No. He invited me in, then when I started asking him questions about the killer he attacked me. Self-defence, sir."

The paramedics rushed towards them. "Whatcha got?"

"He's in there. Stab wound to the groin. I guess he's lost a lot of blood by now; you might want to be quick. Dying would be too good for that arsehole."

The two paramedics cast uneasy glances at each other then dashed inside. After a few minutes he was put on a stretcher and carried out. As he passed Angela he spat at her.

"Bitch," he muttered.

Rather than be disgusted by his parting actions, Angela slid to the floor, the adrenaline rush now dissipating as the events of these last few weeks finally caught up to her. She held her head in her hands and cried, crying for Doug, her brother, everything Kim had been put through. Even Joe who, unable to control his rage, had started this in the first place.

Kim would be fine, eventually, but Doug would never be fine again. He hadn't wanted to get involved with any of this and now he was dead in the very house he swore never to enter again. No doubt she would be interrogated but for now, it didn't matter. At least someone was going to pay for their crimes. If it meant Angela being kicked out of the force, so be it. Kim would appreciate it, anyway.

One of the paramedics attended to the cut on her head then left with one of the detectives keeping an eye on Miles in the ambulance.

"I knew that guy," said an older detective, probably near retirement himself. "Nasty son of a bitch if I remember correctly. You'll have to answer questions, of course, give a full statement, but if he was the serial killer, he won't be leaving prison until he's dead. And good riddance."

To that Angela had to agree.

She told the detectives she had to go pick up her daughter and would make a statement later or first thing next morning. They agreed to let her go after she handed over the jewellery and showed them the rest of Miles' trophies. But before she went to collect Kim from her mother's, there was one last thing to do.

As expected, there were a number of police cars outside 11 Parkland Drive when she arrived. Seeing as she was in her own car, she didn't think she'd be recognised. She parked a little further down anyway, ignoring the neighbours out with their phones recording everything, chatting amongst each other as to what might have happened and stood outside the garden. She looked up at the windows, specifically the one where she had seen her brother that first time. As she stared she thought she saw the vague outline of a figure standing there next to the curtains. It might have been a detective or Joe or Jimmy, she didn't know. She waved anyway, convinced the figure was staring back at her. But the figure didn't respond.

"It's over, Joe. I don't suppose you can ever fully rest or be at peace, but you can stop what you were doing, at least. You can leave my daughter alone now—Miles has been arrested. Time to go, Joe," she said and returned to her car.

Kim rushed to hug her when she arrived at her mother's house. It had been months since she'd received such a heartfelt embrace from Kim, the girl she thought she was losing for good. Tears were shed from all until exhaustion almost caused Angela to stumble in her mother's living room. Pizzas were ordered and it wasn't long before Angela was curled up in her own bed, Kim beside her as though she'd regressed to a young child again. Angela's dreams were peaceful that night. Hopefully, not even Jimmy would visit her anymore although she would never forget him.

---

"It's perfect!" said Maria Hutchinson to her husband Tom and their twelve-year-old daughter, Rebecca. Both were beaming just as she was.

"And I can't believe how cheap it is. This is a dream come true!"

She went outside again, grinning at the freshly painted walls, the garden that looked pristine, not a weed in sight. They could make a real go of it here. The cul-de-sac was quiet, the street clean and well maintained, she still couldn't quite believe how affordable it was. Back up north where they were currently living this would have cost nearly twice as much. Tom could get transferred from the bank he worked at and it was the perfect place to bring up Rebecca. A safe place.

"We'll take it, right?" she asked her husband as he came outside with Rebecca and the letting agent.

"Hell, we'd be stupid not to. Of course, we will. It's even got a basement. I could set up my office down there, or we could turn it into a gym. You should take a look!"

Maria didn't need to be told twice. She dashed off to find the basement, not in the least worried about bugs or spiders down there. The whole house was so clean it looked new, as if no one had ever lived here. She turned on the overhead light and went down the stairs. Tom was right, it was perfect. Spotlessly clean and enough room to live down here if necessary.

"Oh my God, this is so perfect," she muttered to herself again and again like a mantra. Already fantasising about what she was going to do down here, she turned to go back up the stairs when the basement door suddenly slammed shut. Maria screamed, then laughed for spooking herself.

*It was the wind, Maria, get a grip of yourself. Spooky basements only exist in the movies.*

She headed upstairs and opened the door, when she thought she heard a noise behind her. She spun around and was sure she caught a fleeting glimpse of movement in the far corner. Someone giggling conspiratorially.

"Maria Hutchinson, stop it! You'll scare Rebecca," she said, and left to tell the letting agent they were taking the property.

# Acknowledgments

I wrote this book over a year ago; this and another ghost story as yet unpublished, The Helpers. The simple reason it has taken so long to publish is because I had others that I thought had more potential or I was more excited about. I can't remember a lot about this one except I wanted to write a haunted house story that was a little different from the usual. I figured we'd have this house where a number of people have died over the years—nothing unusual there for a ghost story—and they were all murdered by the same person. Naturally, they would want to see justice done.

Then, I had another idea. What if we turned things around a little. A series of unsolved murders at the same time in the same village somehow related to the haunted house? And that was how this story came about. It started out life as a short story; I just added an extra layer to this novel. A lot more work was required on this one because apparently my knowledge of how letting agencies work in England is zero, so thanks to Rachel Eastwood for the tedious job of putting that right. Also, thanks to Heather Ann Larson for going through it again afterwards and adding her own touch to it.

And, as always, thanks to the ARC squad for giving up their valuable time to read an early copy: Carol Howley, Shannon Ettaro, Kristen Gayda, Kate DeJonge, Ali Sweet, Margaret Hamnett, Leah Dawn Baker, Derek Thomas, Jennifer Bauter, Nicole Burns, Donna A. Latham, Corrina Morse, Angel Van Atta, Heather Ann Larson, Tasha Schiedel, Fallon

Raynes, Shannon Zablocki, Samantha Hawkins, Mandy Young, Echo Bennett.

## Also By Justin Boote

Short Story Collections:

*Love Wanes, Fear is Forever*

*Love Wanes, Fear is Forever: Volume 2*

*Love Wanes, Fear is Forever: Volume 3*

Novels:

*Serial*

*Combustion*

*Carnivore: Book 1 of The Ghosts of Northgate trilogy*

*The Ghosts of Northgate: Book 2 of The Ghosts of Northgate trilogy*

*A Mad World: Book 3 of The Ghosts of Northgate trilogy*

Short stories available on Godless:

*Badass*

*Grandma Drinks Blood*

*A Question of Possession*

*If Flies Could Fart*

*Man's Best Friend*—an extreme novella

*Love You to Bits*—an extreme novella

(Both available on Godless and Amazon)

# About the Author

Justin Boote is an Englishman living in Barcelona for nearly thirty years and has been writing horror and dark fiction for approximately 6 years. He spent the first 4 years writing short stories, having around fifty published in a variety of magazines and anthologies before turning his attention to novels. To date he has self- published four short stories, three short story collections, four novels, and a five-book demon/zombie series, The Undead Possession series. He lives with his wife, son, and cat and when he is not writing he is usually thinking about writing, playing Candy Crush, or feeding Fat Cat.

He can be found at his Facebook group https://www.facebook.com/groups/457222379195724

And his website
https://justinboote.com/

Printed in Great Britain
by Amazon